Geographies

stories by
Carmelinda Blagg

atmosphere press

Published by Atmosphere Press

Cover design by Josep Lledo

Atmospherepress.com

Praise for *Geographies*

Geographies, by Carmelinda Blagg, emerges as an exceptional anthology of short stories, weaving a tapestry of human emotion and experience. Within its pages, readers are introduced to a range of vividly drawn characters, each navigating the complexities of love, loss and the intricate dance of human relationships.

–Literary Titan

Through fleeting encounters and lasting impressions, these stories capture the essence of places as ephemeral homes, where the heart finds refuge in unexpected corners.

–L. Hayataka, *Independent Book Review*

[This] is a collection of literary and psychologically astute short works that is highly recommended reading for followers of contemporary fiction; especially those who look for stories rooted in transformation and geographic landscapes of discovery.

–D. Donovan, Senior Reviewer, *Midwest Book Review*

*In memory of my parents, Mary and Woodrow Blagg
and for my beautiful family*

*In fond remembrance of A.D. for believing in me
and loving me*

Table of Contents

Why love what you will lose?
There is nothing else to love.
                            Louise Glück

Love is a deep and a dark and a lonely
and you take it deep take it dark
and take it with a lonely winding
and when the winding gets too lonely
then may come the windflowers...
                            Carl Sandburg

The List

Oh Hallie, I can still see your hands cupping that egg, the tips of your fingers trembling as the chick poked its way through the shell, and then there it was, and the way you looked at it—a little wet pulp of a thing hardly bigger than your thumb. And then, finally, after what felt like forever, you looked up at me, lifted the bleating chick close to me so I could see. You wanted me to see, so I looked. I saw a wet trail of crimson on your lab glove. And the chick's head, its eyes still stuck shut, damp and puffed and blue, like a wounded boxer's.

A miracle, Ben, you said. A whole universe inside a thin membrane.

I felt embarrassed because I thought it was just an ugly chick and that you should put it back in the incubator. But I stayed quiet because we didn't really know each other that well and I was falling in love with you.

We're out of milk, Hallie. I've got to go to the market. Talk about a wounded boxer. That's how I feel this morning. Like my head's a rock someone's been kicking around. Could use some English muffins too, I guess. I'll make a list. You were the one who always started the list. But I'll make the list. I have to. Otherwise, I won't get on to the next thing.

Milk
English muffins
Green grapes (seedless)
Light bulbs (for the bathroom)

I'm using too many bulbs lately. I keep forgetting to turn off the bathroom light at night. You used to do it. I took it for granted that you would. Yes, I know. I took a lot for granted. It's not until I'm in bed that I realize I haven't switched it off, then I don't want to get up, so I just leave it. Sometimes, I wake up because I hear you in the bathroom humming softly, and I can picture you rubbing cream on your face, unpinning your hair as you stand in front of the mirror. Sometimes—I swear—I see your shadow cutting across an angle of light in the hallway.

Oh Hallie, I say before I realize it, please come to bed.

Lunchmeat.

Bread—the loaf I have has molded now. I keep forgetting to put it in the freezer so it will keep.

Mmmm...there it goes...another good, sharp pain in the temples. Makes my eyes hurt. I'll stand still for a minute. Let it pass.

Chocolate chip cookies—you always liked adding these, saying you should always have something on the list you really don't need.

Oh Hallie, why did you have to leave me? Here. Like this. I mean, I'm not angry with you. It's not like that. I just always thought it was me who should go first, because you'd be so much better at this "surviving spouse" stuff than I am. You would look the part, walk the part, act the part. With more dignity and with your wits intact.

But it never works like that, does it? There you are in the hospital, IVs running into the crook of your arm, your face a pale moon, and it's you, you, holding my face in your hands, your thumbs stroking my cheeks, wiping away my tears like

I'm the one who's dying.

You said, Ben, don't be ashamed, and when you said that, it deepened my shame, but I didn't tell you because, of course, I knew you wouldn't understand, and anyway, what good would it have done?

My keys. Where did I put my keys?

Think. Where was the last place you had them?

Now I laugh. I used to say that to you when you'd misplace something, and it always infuriated you.

They're where you left them last, on the table next to the coat rack in the vestibule. Yes, yes.

Dixie cups—for the bathroom. Gosh, Hallie, remember Brooklyn? After the war. Those university days—such heady days, when we were young Marxists. Our immigrant parents weren't amused. You were doing your biology labs with those chicks. I was doing my mechanical engineering classes (a change in my major after my father kept hounding me that a degree in medieval literature would get me nowhere). Remember our group? I guess we were pretty full of ourselves, weren't we? We'd go to Prospect Park, or sometimes we'd take the train to Central Park, spread a blanket on the grass. Willie came, along with Joanna, Stefan, Hans, and others; someone always had a bottle of cheap wine. We'd drink from paper cups, pass around slices of salami and cheese, light one another's cigarettes as we talked—and, yes, argued—about things like dialectical materialism. And Kierkegaard, remember? He was your favorite. I could never get the spelling of his name. It was you who told me his name meant "graveyard" in Danish. Graveyard. Strange, I don't remember much about all those strenuous theories, but this one bit of information about that name stays with me to this day. And all Kierkegaard's anguish about choice, about the kind of dark faith (my term, not yours) that would make Abraham willing to sacrifice his only son, if that's what God wanted. Well, you were the questioning Catholic, I the ethical atheist who would argue—gosh did we ever argue—that my duty would be to protect my son. It wasn't until years later, after Nina and Steven and Carol were born, that I realized how hard it was for you to leave the church. You told me you couldn't believe in it anymore, but as it turned out, it was also just as difficult not believing. You never really gave it up because it was something you knew deep down you couldn't resist. What was it, Hallie? It still pains me that I never actually understood.

It's getting late. I've got to get out of here. The list, get the list.

I get the list. Now the phone is ringing. It's Nina. I pick up and her voice fills my ear.

Her voice. It has that polished sweetness, like someone poking their head through a partly-open door and saying hi. She's got minestrone. And some broccoli-cheese casserole; says she made too much. She asks if she can drop by later and bring me some.

I say of course. I'll be here. Where else would I be?

She'll come, with her Tupperware containers brimming, sealed tight, her smile like yours. She's a good daughter.

Our children, Hallie. We did alright, didn't we? It was you. Mostly you. Somehow, we managed. I always worried, especially when I couldn't untangle my hypocrisy from my anger at seeing them do something foolish or dumb that reminded me of what I used to be like. And I suffered with that. Yes, suffered, through my insistence, my need to always *intervene* (one of your favorite words, that one). I was so sure of myself until I'd run up against you and you would get right up in my face, those lovely green eyes of yours burning into me, threatening me, making me back down. I usually did. You knew I was weak. You found my weakness like a doctor finds a pulse.

It's Nina I worried about the most. The first-born. So nervous. Such a perfectionist. She's always had to put a lot of distance between herself and others. But she took your death hard, Hallie. Didn't go back to her teaching for the rest of that winter semester and the one that followed. I can still see the pain in her eyes. Well, there you are. And now, guess what? She's started going to mass at St. Andrew's. She says she's never felt more at peace. I guess that's good. I imagine you'd be happy about it. Me? I don't know. I can't seem to find a way to talk to her about, you know, the *religious experience*, so we just don't go there.

Steven? He's okay. I guess. Well, *okay* might be stretching it. He and Susan are divorcing. But I suspect you wouldn't be surprised about that. I confess I was afraid of the same thing. He's been trying to make partner for so long, it's just eaten into everything. He works so hard. Did I do that? Is that because of me? I imagine you saying nothing, giving me that smile that says, "Well, what do you think?" Poor Steven. He reminds me of a nervous dog pawing a hole in the backyard to bury his bone, but by the time the hole is dug, he's lost the bone. The last I heard, the kids were pretty upset and Susan has been taking them to a therapist. I think they're too young for that stuff. Steven doesn't like it either, but I'm trying to stay out of it. Still, I wish it were easier to talk to him about things, but it isn't. It never has been, and now, it's even worse since you're not here anymore. I mean, he used to talk to the two of us as if we were one person, but now that you're gone, he can't seem to deal with just me.

Coffee filters—which reminds me. Last week I forgot to put one in while making a pot. I made a real mess. Wet coffee grounds and hot water sputtering everywhere. I could actually hear you scolding me. And I pretended to scurry from you so you'd come after me. I started laughing about that, and then I just felt like an old fool.

Hell, I am an old fool.

Jesus, I miss you, Hallie. It's like not having thumbs.

Carol is happy. Carol really seems to be happy. She's like the child you think about the least who always ends up surprising you. She's still managing the bookstore. Last week she stopped by for a visit. She brings me remaindered titles, old Simenon detective novels and such. And guess what? She told me she's thinking of adopting a child. How about that? I tease her, saying why not do it the old-fashioned way? You know, fall in love, get married, *then* have a baby. But that's not Carol. So I keep quiet because she loves me. I mean, she loves me like she can't help it. It's different from Nina and Steven. They overthink everything. But when Carol sees me, she just throws her arms around me and hugs me so tight, like she's three years old and I'm a tree she's climbing.

Maybe I'll visit the deli and see if they've got any of that corned beef like they had last week. Don't forget your windbreaker, you say. Yes. The weather's fine today, but there's a hefty breeze and clouds are gathering.

Okay, one arm into the sleeve of my windbreaker, then the other. Get my old denim ball cap, punch my fist in the center so it makes a bowl...god, my head hurts. Out of nowhere, another big whooshing pain. I look down at the floor, glimpsing my shoes through a grainy haze. Is that them? I try to put my cap on, but my arm feels numb.

Sit, you say. Sit down for a minute. What's the rush? Oh Hallie, please don't scold me. There's the bench in the vestibule. I want to walk toward it, but my feet feel too heavy. It's okay, you say. It's okay, Ben. You say my name and it feels like you're touching me.

I love the sound of your voice saying my name—like it's something you've owned for a thousand years. It's proprietary, you know. Love. It is. I don't care what anyone says.

I've made it to the bench. I'm here. Feeling a bit lightheaded. My skull is pounding. I reach for the keys, but no sooner do I have them than they slip from my hand, clattering to the floor. A sound that always startled you. Well, it startles me now. Like a sudden clap of thunder.

The phone is ringing again. I hear it like it's miles away. But I can't move, Hallie. It rings and rings.

Never mind, you say. Dammit, Hallie. This is no time for games. Please. Just get the phone.

Ben, you say. Be quiet. Be still. Yes. My back feels very warm, like there's a flame in my spine.

Well, at least the phone has stopped ringing.

I have a memory of something, Hallie. I must tell you. Last week, I was sitting at the dining room table, peeling a tangerine—which reminds me, I need to add tangerines to the list. The list. Where is the list?

Anyway, I looked out through that big window we have in the dining room and I saw two black-capped chickadees. Remember how, now and then, they'd show up, taking us by surprise? They were in the holly, hopping from branch to branch—up goes one, the other comes down, like musical notes. Such nervous rhythms they have. Such hunger. And how small they are. I just couldn't take my eyes off them. And then they were gone. A quick fluttering, and then nothing. So I took the peels from the tangerine. Ridiculous, you'd say, they won't eat those, but I didn't have any seeds. Anyway, I went outside and scattered them around the holly and...

Damn, my head, my neck...a lot of pain. It's okay, you say, just like you're sitting next to me. I've got to get the keys. But I can't move. Except I'm slipping now. Going from the bench to the floor, like an ice cube melting. My rump lands against the floor. It doesn't hurt. I feel like Steven's little girl, Julie, when she was two and trying to take her first steps. Remember? One-two-three, then boom, down she'd go. And how she'd laugh.

Sit for a while, you say. Okay. I won't try to move. I can't anyway. God, I can't believe how tired I am. Yes, you say. I know.

What, Hallie? What do you know? Tell me. Please.

But wait. I didn't finish telling you. About the tangerine peels. I put them close to the holly and...

Hush, you say. Hush now.

It's very quiet here in the vestibule. I push my heel against the tiled floor, but I can't get any traction.

Tangerines

Where are you, Hallie? I wasn't finished saying...the chick-adees came back and took the peels. I don't know when. I tore them into very small pieces so they could take them into their beaks because they're so small...the weight of their bodies, Hallie, hardly...anything.

Geographies

Amelia Island, Florida – 2003

Cut his body open, he thinks, and you would find all kinds of maps inside.

He sits in his blue wingback chair surrounded by boxes. His daughter, Eva, has been busy packing away his books, his photos, and other things, though he hasn't that much left of *things*. Last year he fell—a tumble resulting in a few bruises that bothered her more than him. But now, she fears he cannot live on his own any longer.

Perhaps she is right.

A topographical map of frayed, yellowing silk lies draped across his lap, his knees. It shows the Pyrenees with their jutting, undulating ridges and cartoonish halos of clouds shrouding the tallest peaks. Stains the color of tea freckle across its sheen. He lifts it to the light and sees places where the threads are separating, the blotchy images of mountains and sky. He returns the map to his lap, his palsied finger tracing its lines, remembering the gray winter landscape of France, his stomach flat against the earth, his cheek resting against his rifle. He had fallen to earth, the dome of his parachute spread like a huge apron in the sky.

He remembers the open grave they had ordered him to dig, the clumps of dark, muddy earth on his shovel, his face sweating in the freezing air. He remembers the smell of the earth.

Eva is playing a CD of Mozart's arias, her voice softly echoing the soprano's. She sounds like her mother.

He closes his eyes, drops his head back. He dreams of that open grave, thinking of his escape. Harrowing. The stuff of novels, which he had turned it into. Six years of work. Now it is just a thick manuscript gathering dust.

"Poppi?" Eva touches his shoulder.

He opens his eyes, looks around. Bare windows. The room feels strangely unfamiliar. He looks up at his daughter's face, her quiet eyes, a smile that betrays uncertainty. She has her mother's pale beauty.

"How about a little lunch?" she asks.

He nods. "Did you know when your mother left me, she not only took you and Niels, she took the good silver too?"

Eva drops her face, purses her lips, shaking her head. "Oh, Poppi, that's so long ago! You know how she was. She just couldn't stand being away from Vienna."

"She couldn't stand not inflicting her own kind of punishment."

Eva laughs. "Poppi," she sighs. "Why do you always drag yourself back through all that ancient discord?"

"What?" he says, impatience rising as Eva turns, heads back to the kitchen, singing along softly again, *Exsultate jubilate*. Beautiful B flat above a C.

"I'll make you a sandwich," she says, partly *jubilate*.

"You know I only tell you these things now to make you laugh," he says.

Her voice rises again. She chides him as she spreads mayonnaise on bread, laying slices of turkey and tomato on top.

He looks again at the silk map. The sky is a flat blue, but he doesn't remember any kind of color when he was falling through it. Only his body buffeted by swift winds, his ears burning, the palms of his hands raw from gripping the parachute.

Sonya still remains a bruising mystery. He had met her in Vienna after the war when she was working as a translator for the Allies. She was from Linz. He would watch her at the *Statsopera*. He remembers the backstage vigils, sending elaborate bouquets, numerous wedding proposals before she finally said yes. They were married in a ceremony at the Votivkirche, the church founded by a grateful Franz Josef.

They were happy. It was a world no longer at war. They flew to America. He promised to build a house for them by the sea.

**

He sleeps. It is not yet the future for him. The wound on his thigh has been cleaned and stitched. The torn ends of his skin have not yet fused. The bandage is large and wraps around his thigh like a girdle. His knee is a swollen yellow knot. It is hot in the small hospital room. A window is open, only partly, because it has no screen. There is, occasionally, a breeze, but it is so hot, so stifling it makes breathing painful. His right thigh burns. The pain seeps in through a dense, morphine-induced slumber. It is the kind of pain that stuns him into a deep silence. The hospital is in Naples, and from some of the windows, other soldiers can see Mount Vesuvius calmly rising from a mist in the distance.

He cannot see Vesuvius from where he lies. Beyond his window is a gray building. Lines of laundry hang in startling profusion, row after sagging row of white bedsheets and lace underwear, T-shirts, a man's khaki pants, a woman's cotton scarf that carries a pattern of roses, children's socks that look like the tongues of animals. The building next door was bombed, but this one has remained, and the women still insist on hanging the laundry in the sun.

He remembers a nurse touching his arm, whispering slowly, trying to explain the telegram about his boy. Something has happened.

He gazes out the window as she reads the telegram and he sees the boy running, always running. He runs across a field, wearing dark shorts and a white shirt, arms waving. Gray clouds above block the sun. The landscape is flat and brown and there are trees—fruit trees, pear and apple—that look small against the sky, and in the sky the gray has swallowed the blue. There is that low fence he had built to enclose the orchard, and the boy runs alongside it, his fingers grazing the white wood as he races toward the house. The arrangement of tree and fence and field and sky have become distorted so that everything is smaller and too far away. The boy is too far away; it would not be possible to run after him. Now he cannot see the boy, cannot see how small he is as he loses his footing where the ground slopes suddenly downward. But he remembers where that shallow dip and rise of earth occurs, how easily he would lose his own footing, there, just near the orchard. He knows that before the lightning strikes the boy, he will cut his knee on a sharp piece of rock as he falls, before the force of the lightning throws him, leaving him lying there stunned and motionless out beyond the last pear tree.

The nurse has left the telegram, like a folded handkerchief, on his bandaged thigh. He remembers seeing the words about the boy and about the tree—which he imagined to be the pear tree he planted when they first bought the farm—and about the lightning. There is nothing about the boy's bleeding knee; nothing about the swallows that he knows would have been there, flying mournfully above, fleeing the storm clouds; nothing about the boy's face, startled and mute.

It is not yet the future for him. He remembers the telegram, but was it in the dream? Or did it make the dream? A breeze lifts the telegram and it falls away from his bandaged thigh, floating to the floor.

Now he hears Eva—it must be Eva—moving boxes, muttering and sighing, but it feels as if she is far away and it is only possible to discern the aura of her fretfulness, her disagreeable love.

He remembers one summer here on Amelia Island in this same apartment, many years later. He sits on the balcony watching the sea. Eva is there, sitting across from him, quietly peeling an orange. She asks him about the boy who, had he lived, would have been her half-brother. He is quiet at first, but then, in a low voice, he tells her the facts of what happened. He talks about how the boy tripped, a freakish accident, and then the lightning. Eva listens, nodding, speechless, her mouth drawn down as slowly, carefully, she lays pieces of orange peel in a neat pile on a small glass table between them, his tumbler of bourbon nearby, ice melting in the sun. He remembers the nurse's whispering voice. And the dreams that followed. Always, those birds are there, circling the skies, always that unbidden premonition of how quickly the sky darkened, how the drops of rain gathered, pouring through the trees in the orchard as the boy's breathing ceased.

The sea moves in, retreats, making a sound like breathing, over and over again.

Without a Map

*"The disproportion of the world seems
fortunately to be merely numerical."*
Franz Kafka, "The Zürau Aphorisms"

The Carabinieri officer—nodding with marginal sympathy and smiling tightly—had at least been kind enough to drop Mariel back at her hotel, a roguish gleam in his eye as he acknowledged the unfortunate nature of her situation. He had regretfully pointed out to her that the ratio of purse thieves and pickpockets to tourists in the Eternal City was easily around 3:1, and that, even as he was speaking, some other poor tourist was, no doubt, being separated from his wallet, or her handbag.

A boy had mugged her. A block from the Spanish Steps where she had stood thumbing a guide map. A *little* boy. She didn't see his face because of the sun blocking her vision. But she had felt his assault—a sudden, violent tug on her purse strap that nearly snapped her shoulder joint loose. Then he had shoved her, knocking her down onto the hard lumps of cobblestone.

His small body kept appearing and vanishing in Mariel's

head. She saw him fleeing, the slender strap of her bag thwack-ing against his leg. She tried to maintain a useful snapshot of him in her brain: a dark crop of hair, the tail of a plaid shirt lifting behind him, yellow socks and frayed sandals. But then he seemed to evaporate, over and over.

Now, back at the hotel, Mariel's palms ached. She had wrapped herself in one of the hotel's plush bathrobes before stretching out on the bed. She touched a hand to the ice bag on her left hip, which had turned the color of those iridescent plums she had at breakfast. Her right shoulder ached.

Her husband, Gerald, had greeted her with a look of glazed preoccupation. His face contorted with an expression of dread when she told him what happened. But he didn't seem to know how to touch her. He asked about the credit cards. Yes, they were gone. Everything. Her billfold, the 100 euros, even her phone. He busied himself with calling the credit card com-panies, the phone company. It was a while before she realized he was sweating, his shirt soaked, though the room had an air conditioner that made it feel like a cold storage locker.

She showed him her bruises. He winced, shaking his head. He offered her some Tylenol. He did all this with such an air of distraction that made her glad she hadn't called him from the police station. She could too easily imagine him blaming her for allowing herself to be victimized (she was ahead of him on that count anyway) before ever expressing concern. A familiar, gnawing impatience with him was returning.

Now Gerald was tensely perched at the end of the bed, grip-ping his phone as he scrolled its screen with anxious thumbs. His mouth was tight. He shook his head, now and then closing his eyes.

The TV was on. A large flat-screen fixed to a wall patterned in orange fleur-de-lis wallpaper. A CNN reporter was standing on the shores of Lesbos amid a chaotic scene of men, women, and too many children clamoring from the prow of a tiny boat. The reporter, a skinny fellow in khakis and a rain jacket, was shouting at the camera. Mariel's eyes fixed on the tense quivering of his Adam's apple. Across the bottom, a screen crawl declared a plunge of 400 points in the stock market, followed by something about the arrest of a well-known actress. Mariel winced.

She snatched the remote from the little bedside table, brandished it upward, and pressed the OFF button.

"Gerald, what are you doing?" she said.

He kept scrolling, shaking his head. His mouth was moving, but she couldn't hear his words.

"Gerald?"

He looked up. Gerald was tall and thin, a devoted jogger. He had feet like a platypus, thinning wisps of sand-colored hair, a big, loopy grin. All endearing traits to Mariel. But none of these charms were evident now. He looked a lot like those stunned refugees she'd just seen on the news, pale and pinched with desperation.

He stood, letting his phone slip from his hand and onto the bed. He looked wasted in the opulent room, pacing in front of a pair of tall windows thickly draped in apricot satin. A series of prints of the Vittorio Emanuele monument, the Forum, the Vatican, all in slender gilded frames, adorned the rest of the lemon-colored walls.

"This is bad. This is really bad." He was shaking his head.

Mariel quickly sat up, the ice bag tumbling from hip to floor. She fixed her eyes on Gerald, his naked toes curling against the oriental rug.

"What's wrong?"

He stopped pacing. He plunged his hands into his pockets, shaking his head.

"I'm not sure how to say this…"

"Just say it," Mariel said. "Tell me."

He shrugged. He suddenly looked like a little boy with a terrible secret.

"Um, you want some more ice?"

She glared at him, slowly shaking her head.

"Talk."

He gazed vacantly at his feet.

"Well..." He paused, bunching his mouth, taking a deep breath. "I put quite a lot of money into the market this past year—a lot..." He shook his head, forcing a laugh laced with pain. "Money that was doubling and tripling. It's gone now. Poof." He clapped his hands together dramatically. "If we don't stop the bleeding, it's over."

She stared at him, dry air filling her mouth.

"Stop the bleeding?"

He nodded, looking dazed as he nibbled his lower lip.

"All of it, Gerald?"

He thrust his hands in his back pockets, continuing to pace, nodding then shaking his head. With shoulders slumped, he shuffled past her to the bathroom. She heard the door close, the lock clicking sharply into place.

Damn him, Mariel thought. She felt disaster creeping, like wisps of smoke curling and rising from beneath a door. She untied her robe and quickly dressed, thrusting her legs into her jeans. She knelt and retrieved her sandals from beneath the bed and buckled them on. Her body still ached from the day's earlier assault, but she wanted to get out of there.

She eyed Gerald's wallet on the dresser. She picked it up, sifted through it, pulling out a handful of euros, which she folded and stuffed into the front pocket of her jeans. She closed her eyes, clasping her hands to her chest, whispering *breathe, breathe, breathe.*

All she could see was that reporter's Adam's apple straining up and down.

She grabbed her jacket, the room key.

She heard the toilet flushing as she closed the door behind her, fleeing down the narrow hallway, choosing to take the stairwell instead of the elevator.

**

The sun was a flame on her shoulders. Mariel ducked beneath the canvas umbrellas of the Campo de' Fiori, grateful for the shade. She wandered amid rubber-banded bouquets of spider mums and roses in white buckets, stacked crates of brown pears, sunny lemons, dangling tresses of garlic, huge pumpkins slit open to show their flesh and seeds. Housewives and tourists filled their bags. Mariel liked the amiable bickering and bargaining. Listening to it in Italian made it feel at once distant and intimate. She surveyed the abundance, hands in pockets, a palm wrapped around the folded euros. She eyed a crate of oranges, one or two of them halved and propped to catch the light. Breakfast was hours ago. She was starving.

She bought an orange, a handful of dates, a baguette, a wedge of cheese, a bottle of water. She made her way across the Piazza Farnese, and in the shadows of the Farnese Palace, she found a stone bench and sat. She ate eagerly, crumbs from the bread gathering in her lap. Nearby, a half-dozen warbling pigeons trolled for morsels and she flung a handful of crumbs at them. Some of the birds were so fat they teetered sideways as they walked, partially spreading their wings to keep themselves steady.

Their cat, Bonaparte, would be in heaven here, watching these birds. She pictured him, tensely crouched and ready to pounce. He'd get at least one. One is all he would need. He had a near saintly patience, waiting to take a bird.

She sighed. A creeping dread rose again. Was this the way to do it? Come to a foreign city, book an expensive hotel, behold all the glittering, seductive relics, the stunning beauty of the place, only to realize her fears persisted, like a terrible ringing in her ears.

These days, she likened her marriage to a daisy plucked of its petals, leaving only the flower's eye to contemplate—a yellow button dense with its own complicated structure and, having lost its petals, shining like a bald scalp.

She looked at the pigeons again; she felt herself to have wings, a beak she would use viciously against another bird trying to take more than its share of crumbs. She felt the futility of having a pigeon's claws struggling against the slippery, grimy cobblestones. How it added to the desperation inherent in seeking crumbs.

She looked up. A mime was setting up for his routine near one of the piazza's fountains across from the palace. He was dressed in baggy gold overalls, cradling six white bowling pins with throats banded in red. He knelt and switched on a boom box at his feet. It split the air with the shunting rhythms of hip-hop. He began tossing the pins, one after another, into the air, his pencil-thin body like a quivering dollop of gold leaf in the afternoon sun, the pins arcing in the air and back into his hands. Mariel felt herself to be one of those pins, a red ribbon too tight around her throat, tossed into the air, landing back in the mime's hands before being tossed into the air again. TV images of those refugees ran a loop in her brain—hordes of them in collapsed life jackets circling the reporter, shivering, desperate; an aid worker in the background passing out bottles of water. One child stood beside shrink-wrapped pallets of rations. The Greek Sea was dark and murky, the sky a coral-streaked curtain.

During their flight, just moments after they had ascended to 35,000 feet, she looked down to see Gerald's toes tensely buckling in his sandals. After slugging back one of those two-ounce vials of Johnny Walker, he'd donned a sleep mask and earplugs, but the tips of his fingers had turned white from gripping the arms of his seat. This visceral panic while flying was something new. He said he was just tired, trying to unwind. She wondered what nightmare was erupting beneath his eyelids.

Dear, sweet Gerald with the classic control-freak personality; the brilliant, hypercritical Ph.D. quant who, these days, breaks out in a nervous sweat whenever the NASDAQ numbers appear on a screen crawl. Funny and charming Gerald, who used to imitate an avuncular Einstein sketching his elegant proofs of relativity with a thimble-sized piece of chalk on the sidewalk outside her dorm ten years ago. God, thought Mariel, shaking her head. Those days felt like a hundred years ago.

Now he sifts algorithms, whispering financial mantras as he maps pathways for the flow of money. It makes his eyes glow. He has become a mystery to her.

She watched the pins whirling around the mime. He'd switched to a song with a slower, syncopated beat to match the rhythm of his tossing. He was good. He had a fluid agility that allowed him to look up at the sky, able to trust what the rest of his body could do.

Mariel sighed. Somewhere in this sprawling ruined city, there was a boy with her purse, her digitized biography—encoded, plastic, numeric—emptied onto some table. She imagined him counting the bills, sifting through her things beneath pinched lamplight.

People stopped to watch the juggler now, some holding up their phones, taking pictures. The lone juggler everyone glimpses peripherally as they hurry from one place to another, until someone stops to watch. And then someone else stops. In just a few minutes, the juggler had an audience surrounding him, and all Mariel could see were his pins flying in the air.

And there, amid the growing crowd, she thought she glimpsed a small figure weaving and darting like a mosquito. A dark-haired boy. That same plaid shirt? She sprang to her feet, baguette crumbs and orange peels falling, pigeons fluttering.

She tossed the remains of her snack in a nearby trash can and hurried toward the fountain. The mime was now balancing one pin on his chin while continuing to juggle the others. She thought she saw the boy standing beside a large woman, a mesh shopping bag bumpy with produce slung on her forearm. He was small and quick, just as Mariel remembered. She moved faster now. But by the time she reached the spot where the juggler was, the crowd had started to thicken and she couldn't see the boy or the woman he'd been standing near. She only saw the juggler's pins and lots of arms thrust into the air, hands gripping phones, a crescendo of soft clicks. Mariel stood behind one man, craning her neck, hoping to see something through the screen of his phone, but the sun was so bright she couldn't see anything but a dull glare.

Something brushed her leg. She turned, looking down to see a small terrier sniffing her ankles. He looked up at her with his coal-dark eyes, his body trembling. Someone jerked on his leash and the dog skittered sideways, yelping. Mariel felt her chest tighten at the sight of the poor animal. It scurried along nervously, in thrall of a tall, skinny woman in blue jeans and a leather jacket.

Seconds later, the boy rushed past her. Somehow, he'd materialized out of the crowd. He was running around the fountain. Mariel stepped back, watching him as he came around again, passing her. Her palms were sweating now, but she was determined to wait as he circled again, and after a few seconds, when he did, she stepped in front of him. His cheeks were flushed from running, dark eyes that didn't look up. He deftly sidled out and away from her, as if by instinct, and, quickly, Mariel spun and grabbed the tail of his shirt. He froze.

"You little..." Mariel yelled. But after a few seconds of back-and-forth tugging, he somehow slipped his arms out of the shirt and was gone and she found herself holding the weightless shirt in her hands. Several people in the crowd turned and looked at her, then down at her hands gripping the boy's shirt, then back at her.

Mariel's face burned. She saw the boy traversing the piazza. He disappeared to the left, down a narrow side street, and she ran after him. All the pulse points in her body were pounding. As she went off to the left, where she'd seen him running, the glare of hot sunlight suddenly gave way to shadows cast by ochre-hued buildings on either side of the street. She couldn't see him. She couldn't see much of anything. She stopped to catch her breath, blinking her eyes. A chaotic mingling of voices rose from the end of the street and when she looked up she saw a group of kids bunched around the entrance to a church, kicking a ball back and forth, jumping, yelling, laughing. And then she saw the boy—in his dark blue T-shirt, his shorts, those same scuffed sandals and frayed yellow socks—just as he cut off to the right, disappearing again.

"Damn," Mariel fumed. She kept going, past the church and the yelling kids and onto a familiar street. She recognized the arch with its long tendrils of ivy snaking downward. Via Giulia. She and Gerald had walked through here from their hotel the morning after they'd arrived and had gotten settled in their room. Via Giulia was wide—really more of an avenue— and she suddenly saw herself walking alongside Gerald who was, of course, lost in the labyrinth of market numbers rising and falling from the screen of his phone. She had danced a circle around him, smiling, trying to distract him, hoping to get him to look up, to smile. He'd been nursing a headache from the whiskey he'd had on the plane and a burning gut from the thick, dark coffee the hotel offered at breakfast, and within a span of a few feet, they had ceased talking.

The street was beautiful—neatly swept, adorned and redolent with the hushed polish of wealth. During their stroll that morning, Mariel had observed an elderly woman in a smart blue suit crossing the street, one hand shading her eyes from the bright sunlight, the other gripping an expensive-looking shoulder bag, and Mariel had felt very *undressed* in her blue jeans, her T-shirt, her lumpy backpack. The next day, while ambling through an outside market, she spotted a hive of leather handbags dangling from a hook, caramel-colored and gleaming against the bright blue sky, and she bought one for herself. It was the same purse the boy had stolen from her.

Now she spotted him racing through some iron gates to the entrance of a church—pale marble, richly carved pillars— where he vanished behind a pair of tall green doors. When she reached the church, she stopped, struggling to catch her breath. Her feet ached in her thin sandals. The straps around her ankles stung her skin. She rubbed her bruised and still-swollen hip and groaned softly. She looked down at her hand, still gripping the boy's shirt.

She went up to the doorway of the church and peeked in. It was cool inside, tiny rows of votive candles flickering in the small, dimly lit nave. A large painting in a gilded frame hung from the back wall of the nave, glowing with angels and saints. She felt a familiar longing, touring these beautiful old churches; a longing that cut against her tame agnosticism.

She watched as tourists and worshipers trod softly, though Mariel couldn't see the boy. She decided it wouldn't be a good idea to storm the church and collar him. At least she'd finally caught up with him. She'd wait for him to come out.

She only wanted back what the boy had taken from her. Taken? How about stolen?

Across the street, she saw a couple and their three kids milling around the entrance of a posh residence, its façade covered by lush ivy and trails of rosy bougainvillea. The woman, clad in aqua capris and a bright pink T-shirt, was standing in front of a massive wooden door with a polished brass knocker. She was waving and calling to her husband, who was taking pictures of the kids—two teenage girls and a small boy—with his phone. The kids stood, arms spread across one another's shoulders, in front of a row of clipped boxwoods and a terrace with lemon trees in terra cotta pots.

"Hey hon," the woman shouted. "Get one of me here. I can tell everyone this is our new house." She laughed. The husband swung around to face her, clicking away. The kids hooted.

The sight of the family pulled at her. Ever since she and Gerald had arrived, he'd hardly looked up to notice anything.

Not a statue, not a painting, not a fountain. The city was like a gilded cage in which he paced, back and forth, worrying, while Mariel had too often succumbed to the turbulent, subterranean pull of all those apocryphal images of suffering and resurrected Christs, downcast Virgin Marys, somber-looking saints, beheaded martyrs, and the cheap souvenirs—glittering snow globes with tiny figures of waving popes, the garish T-shirts, jeweled rosaries, crucifixes.

A couple of doors down from the house where the family was, a portly shopkeeper emerged from his small antiques shop gathering items he'd set out on the sidewalk earlier; a couple of mirrors with ornate gold frames, blue and white ceramic vases, a pair of French dining chairs with seats of burgundy silk.

Mariel smoothed the boy's shirt again. Maybe she should just go back to the hotel.

Then, voices again, this time a drift of Italian, soft and melodic, and she turned to see two nuns in their black and white habits emerging from the shadows of the church. One led the way; the second was gripping the hand of the boy and a third nun followed, holding his other hand. They stood outside the doorway and the boy was looking up at them and then he looked at Mariel, and Mariel's eyes locked with his. She glared at him, but his gaze slipped hers, wandering down to where he saw the shirt crumpled in Mariel's hands and suddenly he yelled, pointing at Mariel.

"*Mia camicia! Mia camicia!*"

The nuns turned toward Mariel in unison, protectively flanking the boy. They glared at her and her face grew warm as she unfurled the shirt, waving it like a white flag before letting it drop to the pavement.

The nun on the left stepped forward and picked up the shirt. She held it as she looked at Mariel. "*Perche?*" she said softly, tipping her shrouded head quizzically, her face a mass of pale, soft wrinkles.

"He stole my purse," Mariel said meekly. The nun frowned, shaking her head—either she didn't speak English or hadn't caught what Mariel said, and Mariel, feeling the heat of the nun's eyes on her, kept quiet. The nun muttered something else in Italian, a phrase laced with what sounded like the names of several saints.

Mariel spoke no Italian beyond what her phrasebook could supply, but she had recognized that one word—*perche*. The nuns shook their heads in unison, unsmiling, muttering softly to one another. The boy had gone silent, looking down at his shoes.

The nun with the boy's shirt held it as he slipped his arms in, and then the four of them turned and walked quietly away. He was still between two of the nuns, gripping their hands as the third one led the way up the Via Giulia. Now and then, he'd swing his arms up with the nuns and do a happy hop and skip. Mariel stood, watching and waiting, arms crossed, counting softly to twenty as she tapped a finger lightly in the crook of one arm.

Little scoundrel, she thought.

She followed them, keeping a sufficient distance. No need to run now. The boy might be fast, but the nuns were older and walked the knotty cobblestones cautiously in their heavy shoes. Mariel wasn't wearing her watch, but she figured it was well into the lunchtime hour with the sun still high and warm. After a few minutes, the nuns and the boy paused in front of a church, and Mariel stopped too, stepping sideways into shadow as one of the nuns pointed up to a frescoed panel above the entrance—a white bird with wings spread, flanked by saints, a background of celestial blue pocked with flaking gold stars. From here they turned north, onto a little street that snaked past postcard trees and souvenir offerings jutting out from shop doors, past tiny cave-like workshops where seamstresses and cobblers busily stitched and hammered; past a bar that hummed with the efficiency of waiters in white jackets pouring glasses of iced Campari as pigeons swooped and glided through the dusky shadows and ribbons of sunlight and cyclists whizzed smoothly by in both directions with the velveteen ease of billiard balls sent scattering by the precise, shunting force of the cue stick.

It occurred to Mariel that she was being ridiculous. The whole day had been full of bad news, their vacation now mostly ruined.

They stood in bright sunlight again, waiting to cross the Corso Vittorio Emanuele where a densely-packed tour group was fast advancing from the other side of the Corso, a herd into which the boy and the nuns appeared to dissolve.

The Corso buzzed with traffic, and Mariel could no longer see the foursome. She anxiously zigzagged across. It was more crowded on the other side of the Corso, but through the throngs of people, Mariel spotted the nuns and kept walking until she found herself standing at the juncture of another familiar little street she and Gerald had walked that morning.

She looked to her left and saw the nuns walking arm in arm, now on the fringes of another tour group. But the boy was no longer with them.

He was like smoke, a cloud, a bird that darts freely, elusively, through forests of thick trees.

She wasn't far from their hotel—the last place in the world she felt like going.

But she walked up the little street that she knew led to the hotel anyway, as if in a film running backward, and she began retracing her steps to the hotel, recalling that this street dead-ended into another where she and Gerald had gotten slices of pizza on their way back from the Via Giulia and where, for once, Gerald had noticed something that amused him. The unusual successive numbering of the street that ran in a circle, from low numbers on the left to high numbers on the right. What was it he had said? Something about a vector returning to its point of origin, only oriented in the opposite direction; a circle whose path takes an odd turn.

She felt like the blue dot on a Google map, turtling along, unable to discern if she was following her own shadow leading her forever in a circle. She looked behind her to see if the boy might be following her now—impishly lampooning her pursuit of him.

But when she turned back, there he was. Or was it him? Just past the entrance to the bar where she and Gerald had gotten their pizza, she saw a boy, the same small, spare frame, but this boy wore jeans and a white T-shirt. Blocking his path was a large woman, soiled apron, breasts like melons, thick arms. She loomed, frowning, gesturing madly as the boy froze. The woman dug a hand into his shoulder, shaking him. She grabbed one of his ears between her fingers, twisting it as she rained curses on him until he doubled over, wincing, groaning. This was a scene to be watched, to take in for the theater it was, and no one moved. Some people didn't even appear to take notice. And while it felt to Mariel that it was going on forever, it happened quickly as the woman, roughly ushered the boy inside the shop from which Mariel pictured her emerging, like a sea creature from its shell. Above the door, it read *Tabacchi*.

From the darkened shop the screams continued—the woman's fury, the boy's wailing, restaurant patrons and shoppers nervously laughing or warily shaking their heads. Mariel felt stupid and small. Hearing the boy's cries made her stomach contract like a muscle in painful spasm. She stood now on the street, trying to conjure a mental map that would take her back to the hotel. She walked past the elegant storefronts that breathed out the occasional gust of cool air, the little cafes, the boy's cries still in her ears.

Then someone gripped her elbow and Mariel gasped. Her eyes grazed the cobblestones where she saw Gerald's big feet and toes in the footbed of his sandals, the reddish coils of hair on his shins.

"Where've you been?" he said. She looked at him, then down at his hand, now closed tightly around her forearm.

"What's going on?"

She shook her head, blinking in confusion. His fingers dug into her arm.

"Why'd you run off?"

His face had that familiar lopsided grin, but his eyes were wide with a kind of manic agitation.

"What's wrong?" he said. But Mariel couldn't speak. He was still gripping her arm, and it was hurting now. "Did I scare you about the money? I'm sorry. Everything will be okay. I can fix it," he said. "You might have left a note..." He paused. "I mean, for a minute there you had me thinking the worst."

Mariel wrestled her arm away with a jolting eruption that rippled through her body and nearly sent her tumbling to the cobblestones. Gerald reeled backward and for a few seconds they faced one another, like tottering wrestlers.

"No," she whispered.

He reached for her again, but this time, she put a hand on his chest and shoved him. His pale face looked like a dumb white moon.

She started running—away, away, away from him, feeling as she did her heart coming up through her throat, warm air filling her shirt, bathing her skin.

"God, what's gotten into you?" This time his voice was shaking.

She kept going, kept moving down one snaking side street after another, stepping across angular pools of shadow and sunlight without a map.

Slipstream

Eva thought she was leaning toward *no*. What would change if she said yes? Married or not, Anders would always be in her life.

The night before she left Vienna to come here, he had presented her with a ring. Platinum with three small diamonds. He pressed it into her palm, saying it was time they gave marriage a go. She let him slip it on her finger, not knowing what to say. After all these years, he'd left her feeling dumbstruck. Later, as she finished packing her suitcase, she slipped the ring into her handbag. On the plane, as the sight of land gave way to water, she took it out again. It was a lovely brushed platinum, the tiny diamonds glinting like flecks of ice. She felt a thorny pleasure, slipping it back on her finger before returning it to her bag.

From the apartment's small living room, she heard the faint ripple of her father's snoring. Draped over one knee was the square of frayed silk she recognized as one of his escape maps from his days as a paratrooper during the war. He wore one of those shirts—the kind sold in little *surf shacks*, as they were called around here. Eva saw it was buttoned crooked and coffee stains had survived laundering. His breathing sounded rough. This morning at breakfast, he looked as if he hadn't slept, though he'd insisted otherwise. His doctor was not happy with his blood pressure numbers.

She eyed his lunch plate, the half-eaten sandwich she'd made him, resting on his thigh.

"Poppi?" she whispered as she pulled up the ottoman and sat down beside him. The apartment was almost empty now. Down to the—what was the word her father had used—something like a *nub*? Her father, with his dry humor, his protean energies now waning at the age of ninety-two, had finally admitted that a move was *probably* inevitable. Last spring, he took a nasty tumble down the wooden stairway that led from his balcony to the shore, fracturing an ankle. It was still healing, with two screws in place and unsightly scars on his right knee and his chin. He grumbled about using a cane.

On the floor near the chair, she eyed a large atlas of very old maps. How had she missed packing this? She picked it up, placed it on her knees.

"Poppi, wake up."

She took his right hand in hers and placed two fingers on the rise of intersecting veins at the wrist, searching out a spot where she could discern his pulse, rapid and fluttering erratically.

His eyes blinked open. "Am I dead yet?" he said.

She smiled. "Oh, I don't think so," she said.

"I was dreaming," he said.

"About...?"

"The hospital. Naples."

Eva nodded, squeezing his palm. She picked up the silk map, frayed and flecked with sepia-tinted spots. As she held it in front of her, he reached his fingers out and grazed the bottom.

"This one's a favorite," he said. "I have to keep it. It's British."

Eva folded it into a neat and nearly palm-sized square and

placed it in his hands.

"Of course," she said. "How about something to drink?"

He nodded and faintly smiled. "A little scotch and soda?"

"It's a bit early for that, isn't it?"

"Never," he quipped. He patted the arm of his chair. "So, are you going to pull the chair out from under me next?"

She put the atlas down, stood, and cradled his face in her hands, his big jowls like soft pillows, his freckled skin scarred in places where they'd sliced away melanomas.

"Silly goose," she said.

He regarded her with sunken blue eyes.

She returned to the kitchen, rinsing their lunch dishes as she thought again of Anders' proposal. She was married once, in her twenties. He was a violinist from Prague. It lasted less than five years and she swore she'd never marry again; especially a musician. As for Anders, it seemed almost beside the point. He'd been married twice himself and claimed both marriages had failed because neither wife was a musician. Eva was fifty-one now, Anders nearly a decade older; their daughter Liesel would turn sixteen in the fall (she could only imagine Liesel's reaction, having *married parents*). Since quitting his chamber group last year, Anders seemed adrift, filled with energy yet anxious and moody. Then he started calling her with a frequency that felt edged with desperation.

She smiled, remembering when she was the desperate one.

Why marry now? She liked single motherhood. At first, the idea had really scared her, almost as much as being in love with Anders did. But she was a good mother. And Liesel was great—well, most of the time she was. Eva had worked so hard over thirty years—giving concerts, touring with chamber groups and orchestras, making recordings. Two years ago she retired from the rigors of performing concerts and recitals. The time had come and she felt ready. She did the occasional recital, but mostly her days were filled now with teaching master classes in vocal technique and coaching Liesel in the intricacies of lieder.

And really, things were sweeter with Anders now. They had a lovely daughter. They had reached a balance that felt right to Eva. The idea of marriage made her feel superstitious, as if she were tempting fate.

A cockroach skittered from behind the coffee canister. The exterminator said spraying would rouse them and any she saw wouldn't be around very long. For three days, Eva packed boxes, emptied closets, dispatched a load of furniture to Goodwill, and helped arrange things with the staff at Alta Mira Senior Living for moving her father into a small downstairs apartment. The view wouldn't be as good as here, but it would be easier to get around, with doctors available, and still close to the ocean. And, as she repeatedly tried to emphasize, it's *not* a nursing home. It's what they call "assisted living," she said—an annoying euphemism as far as he was concerned.

"I've heard of it," he had said, waving her off. "It's marketing lingo. All soft corners and blurred edges. You forget, I worked on Madison Avenue for fifteen years."

Eva mixed his drink—tipping the soda a bit more than the scotch—and took it to him. He noisily gulped it, dropped his head back and exhaled dramatically, then frowned, claiming she'd obviously forgotten the scotch.

She sat and took the book of maps again in her lap. Its spine was loose and fragile, its folios like two serving trays hinged together. *Mercator's Maps*, the cover read. She thumbed its pages, saw where the continent of Africa lay suspended between the South Atlantic and the Indian Ocean. Birds skimmed the ocean's surface, whales and dolphins and sea serpents bobbed from beneath, and large merchant ships with billowing sails crossed paths.

"Very useful maps," he said.

She looked up. "Mmmh?"

"Long ago. If you were on a ship at sea, you bet."

His face grew lively and alert.

"He made the world a two-dimensional one," he said as he

waved a shaky finger across the page. "Things look different, he distorted the size of places, but if you were sailing a big ship long ago, you could trust his coordinates."

Her father loved maps. The silk ones he used as a pilot, wall maps, street maps. During the war, they were a lifeline, he once said. You simply couldn't afford not to know where you were.

She closed the book. "Well, I won't pack this. Take it with you."

Eva rose. She started to put a hand over his, but then, her father suddenly announced, glaring, that he wanted to stay.

She took his empty glass, thinking of what Maman told her before she left about how stubborn her father could be. She put the book on his lap, but as she started for the kitchen, he reached for her hand, gripping her wrist.

"I'm one bout of pneumonia away, you know."

She sighed. "Oh, Poppi," she softly scolded. "Do you know how silly that sounds?"

Eva had always believed her father was about as helpless as a well-equipped battleship. Though lately, especially after his fall, he'd slowed down, moved more cautiously, shuffling more instead of walking, and the sudden changes had taken Eva by surprise. Perhaps it was his sturdiness, his impervious solidity that she really wanted to protect.

"Where's your brother?"

"Niels is in Linz." Niels, who told her he'd like to help, but with his teaching, the kids, his lab work, his wife nursing an ulcer and four months pregnant, he didn't have time. At least he had agreed to keep an eye on Maman.

"He's busy, Poppi. But if you want to talk to him, we can..."

He turned his attention back to Mercator's maps, his hands shaking as he lifted its pages.

"By the way, that wasn't a real scotch and soda," he said. "Can we try again?"

** *

Eva watched her father grip the stair rail with one hand, his cane in the other, as he stooped to inspect a potted coleus drooping in the midday heat. He had donned the Panama hat she gave him when he turned ninety-one, last year. She had a straw hat too, which she kept in the tiny spare bedroom that's always been hers in summers past. She slipped it on and grabbed the apartment key.

"Needs water," he said, a thumb caressing a maroon-colored leaf.

"I'll do it later," Eva said, closing the door behind her and locking it.

He straightened, turned, and started down the stairs. Eva hurried to catch up to him, slipping an arm beneath his. A sudden gust of hot breeze, salty and humid, whipsawed around them as they continued down the stairs. When they reached the bottom, Eva halted and slipped off her sandals, digging her feet into the sand and sighing at the pleasurable feel, how it almost burned but was so soft that the warmth traveled upward.

She laced her arm through her father's as they strolled. A silence settled between them—a kind of shy father-daughter silence that always reminded Eva of the gaps, the missing years, the distances she and her father had to bridge when their lives long ago diverged. But the moment always came— like a much-needed breath—when the familiarity of his dry humor, his cranky sweetness, his overbearing ways, his chiding affection, all surfaced and her father became *Poppi.*

He stopped, lifted his hat, and fanned himself with it as he squinted up at the sun, running a palsied hand across his bare scalp. "How's my Liesel? Why didn't you bring her?" he said, still not looking at her. "Or have you already told me?"

"Yes," Eva said, squeezing his arm.

"Her father's turn to worry about her?"

"It is," Eva said. "She's doing the Schubertiade this summer, readings and a master class. Anders is taking her."

He nodded, beaming, then his face soured into a frown as he leaned on his cane. "I want a recording. Send me something, will you?"

"Of course, of course..." Eva said.

"I hadn't realized she was so far along."

"Oh dear, she knows lieder better than I did, Poppi. And she's got boys on the brain. *And* she's driving me nuts. She has a very strong will. So I decided to let her father try to keep up with her for a while."

"By the way, you checked your voice messages? From Anders?"

The wind was still gusting warmly, lifting waves as Eva raised her hat, letting the breeze riffle her hair. She tilted her face to the sun. It would, again, likely reach the high thirties today, she thought as she quickly corrected herself to think in Fahrenheit instead of Celsius.

"Yes." She stopped, knelt on the sand to scoop a large fragment of seashell, ashen-colored, striated with darker whorls. "He wants to get married," she finally said.

Poppi cupped a hand over an ear. "What's that?"

"Married," Eva repeated, louder. "He wants to get married."

"Hah!" her father chortled, halting. He lightly patted her hand. "Hope you're not expecting your old man to give the bride away."

Eva humphed. "Oh...stop already."

Another long silence as a trio of gulls descended, skittering to shore, wings flapping as a small boy in red swim trunks and brandishing a broken tree branch chased them.

"I think he's a very fine cellist," her father said, grinning tightly.

Eva took note of the coolly measured distance her father always maintained when it came to Anders. She took his arm again. "I liked it that he asked me. He treated it like a real proposal, ring and all. But, well," she shrugged, "after all these years…"

"Mmm…"

"He quit his chamber group last year. He does some solo recitals, he teaches and tutors."

"Ah…well," said her father, "either he's having an overdue mid-life crisis or he really means it."

She pinched his arm.

"Ouch!"

"Enough."

"I wouldn't know. I am not a modern man. I'm just an old chauvinist. Not to mention an utter failure at marriage. Three times."

Another long silence. Eva felt the hot sun on her back.

"Anyway, tell Liesel I want her to come next time. Tell her Opa is almost in diapers and he'd like to see her."

Eva shook her head. "Not sure she'll believe the part about diapers."

"Give her a guilt trip. Never fails."

"Worked for you, right?" Eva gently poked an elbow against her father's ribs.

They drifted closer to the water where a wave surged forth, skimming the tops of their feet before receding. The water felt cool on Eva's naked feet as she watched her father's shoes get soaked. He didn't seem to notice.

"I missed you something awful, you know," he told her. "Guilt was all I had."

Maman still had his letters, tucked away in a shoebox on a shelf in her closet. Over a dozen of them—pleadings inked in blue or hammered from his Olivetti in the year when it had become clear they weren't going to be a family anymore. Eva once asked her why she kept them. Maman waved away her question with a wistful half-smile.

It was all there in her dark eyes.

"She took you and Niels and just…just like that," her father said, snapping his fingers, seeming to lose his words. "You were both so small."

Eva felt dumb with silence. Her father stood, his shoes, his ankles, his shins all getting soaked by the returning tide. He glared at the horizon.

"It couldn't be helped," he said. "I know I was terrible, too involved in the work, leaving it all to her, throwing money at problems that money couldn't solve."

Eva could feel it. The shift that brought the distance; that brought the past front and center like a lively ghost dancing on the shoreline before them.

She wanted to say that Maman just wanted to go *home*. Vienna was her *home*. Music was her life. But the waves were roaring, and she'd already told him that.

"And it was two pieces of really fine silver she took," he continued, as if the waves rushing toward him could hear. "A serving fork and a ladle. I found them in France. Paid a bundle of francs for them. For us...I got them for us."

**

Maman used to say—with dramatic flair—their family had been made from war. War and the arias of Verdi, Puccini, Bizet, and Tosca.

The war, she added, left its shadows in everything.

Eva had asked Maman where they were going all those years ago on a sun-washed morning in late June, her small suitcase at her feet, a coloring book of dolphins and whales her father gave her tucked beneath her arm. It was 1958 and Eva was six. Her father had kissed them goodbye at the airport, promising he would see them later that summer when he would come and take them home. The trip had been agreed upon as a kind of truce, though that word was never used. Between the ever-frequent quarrels, her father quietly hoped that with a little time and some distance Maman would miss their life in New York.

WIEN her mother had written on the inside cover of Eva's coloring book. The word looked as small as it sounded when her mother pronounced it. Eva had heard her say the word often and her voice always sounded heavy with melancholy.

"It's Maman's home," she had whispered in her thickly accented English, hands trembling as she spoke while braiding Eva's hair and spoon-feeding Niels, barely two.

"You know it won't be the same," her father had warned. "You remember what it was like when we left."

Their plane touched down in Vienna in a gray and hazy dawn and Eva always thinks of that arrival like hearing the sounds of dissonant music interrupted by monochromatic silences.

Poppi had been right. Though Maman would never concede, even as her eyes brimmed with tears when she saw all the modern new architecture, the new bakeries and shops and clothiers, the newly paved *Ringstrasse*. Still, she went in search of places she knew she wouldn't find, as if she needed to convince herself they were no longer there. Her favorite café, the *shuhladen* she'd known since her early school days. Yes, still gone. "Scar tissue," she would say whenever she found traces of something that hadn't been completely erased. But she did find Doblinger's, where she used to get sheet music. The sight of its etched glass doors and windows, its big gold lettering, stunned her into a damp silence. The Imperial Hotel—a place Maman came to loathe—where Hitler had once presided, was again a luxury hotel. A fact that made most Viennese shrug indifferently. They could hardly afford one of its posh rooms.

Three years earlier, Austria had been declared a newly independent sovereign country. Yet, when the war ended, it was the return of the waltzes of Strauss, the Weiner Symphoniker playing Schubert on the Ringstrasse, that had mattered more than anything. And the reopening of the *Staatsoper*. Though it had suffered in the bombings, it had a new façade and a newly gilded interior, and evenings there were often packed from orchestra pit to the highest rafters with Viennese hungry to hear arias whose refrains they knew by heart.

From Vienna they would travel to Linz, where Maman's Aunt Sophie lived. Cousin Gerhardt, Aunt Sophie's nephew, met them at the airport and gathered them onto a train to Linz. From his pockets, he pulled coin-sized discs of chocolate, pressing two into Eva's palm and winking. He held Niels, lifting him high in the air, then holding him close. Maman and Gerhardt talked all the way to Linz, Niels dozing in Maman's lap. Eva understood nothing of what they were saying. She could hear the voice tones—her mother's high and lilting and happy, Gerhardt's deep and low, but with warmth. From her window seat, Eva watched Vienna's urbanscape give way to the thick forests and farmland of the Danube Valley as she unpeeled the gold foil from one of Gerhardt's chocolate discs and shyly nibbled. The northern air of Austria, even in summer, was nothing like America, the sun much farther away, it seemed, its light pale and thin.

Aunt Sophie's hands, soft and wrinkled, gently cradled Eva's face, sunlight raked the cold marble floors of the vestibule where Gerhardt set their suitcases down; from Aunt Sophie's kitchen, the warm smells of a lemon cake. Eva watched as Maman embraced Aunt Sophie, both women weeping. This would become home and *home* would become *zuhause, hiemat, aufenthalt.*

Poppi came later that summer with gifts—pearl earrings for Maman, a silver bracelet for Eva with her name engraved, stuffed animals for Niels. She could see the change in her father's face and in all the ways Maman had already decided. Quietly. She was staying. With the children.

Her father tucked away his hurt pride, his hopes. When Eva hugged him, thanking him for the bracelet, it was longer than usual before he let go. Maman kept rubbing her palms together, struggling to explain that yes, of course, she loved

America, but she could not...or would not...or did not want to go back. She seemed to stumble through her words as her tongue reclaimed the language of her childhood and as Eva watched her, listening to her half-English, half-German pleas, she thought of the evening Maman had taken her to the *Staatsoper* to see *Fidelio*. She remembered seeing her mother's face streaked with tears as the curtain rose on the first act. Was that the moment she decided she would not return to America? Or was it when her mother was silently mouthing the lyrics during the final duet when Leonore had at last saved her husband Florestan from imprisonment and murder? Eva thought of her mother's tears as part of a larger unhappiness she couldn't live without.

On a morning one week after her father arrived, her parents embraced, but then a couple of days later, he had to leave. There were more arguments, more silences, more misunderstandings, little in the way of explanation, as if what couldn't be resolved collapsed into a deafening silence. Eva wept into her pillow, in a bedroom with flowered wallpaper.

What had happened to them?

Home became Linz. *Home* became music. Eva learned to sing the etudes and lieder of Schubert as Maman coaxed her voice, teaching her to breathe and feel the songs in her throat, her palate, the chambers and spaces where breath and body made a voice, embellished by the ornament and trills of *coloratura*. Every day for the rest of her life, music in one form or another—Mozart, Ravel, Bach, Strauss, Schubert, Bizet.

Over the years, a rhythm established itself around her father's erratic transatlantic visits. One August, he took them to a bird festival in a tiny Italian village called Sacile. It had a river running through it, like the Danube that ran through Linz. Tourists and bird lovers came from all over Europe to hear the chorus of birdsong, which would erupt across the dim pre-dawn sky. They went to a bird market where they saw parakeets, macaws, love birds, canaries. Eva and Niels gathered feathers scattered along the streets and around the colorfully tented market stalls—blue ones, green ones, red and yellow ones. Her father took the quilled ends of two deep blue macaw feathers touched with yellow, and with the same pocketknife he had carried with him as a paratrooper, he snipped their ends at an angle, then shaved and shaped them into fine points and made a slit down the middle of the point. He was making pens for them, he said, so they could write to him. As he worked, making little piles of quill shavings, he told Eva and Niels how, during the war, the pilots used homing pigeons to send messages by way of tiny capsules tied to their legs. They would put them in paper bags and drop them from the bomber planes, and the birds would burst from the bags, taking flight in what he called a slipstream. *Slipstream.* She and Niels had bungled the pronunciation of the word. Poppi got a bottle of India ink, dipped the feather in, and, on a piece of hotel stationery wrote the word *slipstream* as Niels ran circles around their hotel room, a shopping bag on his head, flapping his arms like wings and yelling *swipstweam...swipstweam.*

Eva took the word apart, thinking of *slip* plus *stream*, then tying them together, and it became an oddly beautiful word to her, especially when she pronounced it with a whisper.

Time stretched in strange directions, the seasons expanded, contracted—something Eva felt in the shifting patterns of the northern climate and in a new language, where she could still faintly hear the familiar phonic echoes of English in words like *staat* and *state*, *garten* and *garden*, *platz* and *plaza* and *place.*

As a child, you go where you are taken. The world rearranged itself into time zones and the meanings of separation, departure, distance, and in that period between one place and another, one language and another, Eva kept losing things— her woolen coat on the train seat at the station in Linz, her favorite blue sweater at the hotel in Sacile, a pair of sandals and some books in Urbino where she and her father toured the sixteenth-century Ducal Palace and he told her his favorite story of how the Duke lost an eye in a jousting match, a misfortune the nobleman ruefully claimed had made him more insightful.

She kept the quilled pen in a dresser drawer, wrapped in tissue, nestled alongside some scarves—a thing too weightless and delicate to bring with her on her travels.

In the end, what became so permanent, so real, were all those elusive, inexplicable moments; moments of possibility, of waiting; moments where Eva imagined herself standing at an airport gate or the platform of a train station, either anticipating *departure* or *arrival*—a needle in a compass forever fixing its direction.

**

They drove to a restaurant in Fernandina Beach, a favorite place of her father's, where dinner was shrimp scampi and white wine for her, a steak and a beer for her father. They sat outside at a small table on an upstairs deck that looked out over the ocean.

As he finished his steak, he announced—yet again—he wasn't moving. He would get someone to come and help him. She reminded him he'd already driven off two nursing aides.

"This is *home* for me," he said.

"The apartment, Poppi. The roaches...and those stairs..."

"I don't care. It's still home. *My* home." His right hand was trembling, closed into a fist he rested his chin upon as he stared down at a glistening piece of fat on his plate.

"The security deposit's already been paid," she said.

"It's a few hundred dollars. I'll get it back." He looked like a child whose face was melting into old age.

The air was humid and smelled of the sea and charred meat as Eva watched the white-capped waves in the darkening evening. She sighed. She looked at him, smiling stiffly.

"So," her father said. "How about that marriage proposal? You saying yes?"

Eva reached into her handbag, pulled out the ring, and slipped it on her finger. Then she lifted her hand and waved it at him. "I don't know. But I think I'll keep the ring."

He smiled wanly, his face, those heavy jowls, relaxed.

"Such ambivalence. Back in my day..."

"I know," she said, cutting him off.

He scooped a forkful of baked potato into his mouth.

"Poppi, would you...I mean, I've...would you marry Maman, again?"

He did a kind of funny blink-blink with his eyes as he swallowed.

"Why would you say such a thing?" he finally said.

She drank the last of her wine, regarding him with a sideways glance and shrugging. Maman was number two, but Eva always had the feeling Maman was *the one*.

"Would you?"

There was a sheen of melancholy in his eyes. "Yes," he said at last. "I would." He nudged his plate forward with a finger. "Even though we failed. And we'd likely fail again."

From the dim twilight, their waiter appeared, taking up their empty plates as the two of them smiled politely, refusing dessert.

"Coffee?" asked the waiter. As her father nodded, Eva shook her head. The waiter vanished. Her father shifted in his chair and took his wallet from his back pocket. He opened it and carefully teased forth a four-inch square photograph. He set it down between them and Eva looked at it. The photo was fading to sepia, but she recognized a younger Poppi, tall and handsome in uniform, standing with his arm around a very thin woman—that face, that smile, Eva thought. Her dark hair was pinned up, hands defiantly on her hips. She was wearing what looked like a pair of soldier's khakis, much too large—it couldn't be. Eva could make out a background of rubble and ruin behind them.

"That's Maman? She's so skinny. I've never seen this picture."

"The war had just ended. This was taken before I went back to propose. She was a typist and translator for the Allies. Most of Austria was starving then. Yes, she was skinny as a reed, but I don't know, she left me breathless, doing what she could to help people, and risking a great deal. She'd lost her own parents. I nearly lost a leg before I found myself with shovel in hand, being ordered to dig my own grave." He laughed, shaking his head. "We could barely talk to each other—if it hadn't been for the French we both spoke and the smattering of English she knew—but we knew what we had survived. We were alive."

The waiter brought coffee for her father and he asked for the check.

Eva stared at the photograph, that image of Maman.

"She was beautiful, Eva."

She still is, Eva thought.

"I always said she was tougher than I was," he continued. "All sorts of warnings rung in my ears. I'd already ruined one marriage. But I didn't care. Neither of us did. What followed felt as natural as breathing." He paused again. "Seems crazy, doesn't it?" He laughed, shaking his head. "It isn't. War changes everything." He folded his big hands over Eva's. "And anyway, happy endings work better in the movies."

Eva's fingertips grazed the spot between her father's palm and wrist, where she could feel his dancing pulse.

******

Eva lay awake in the dark, a slender, milky rectangle of moonlight shining on the floor. She'd never known her parents as two people in love.

She thought of calling Munich. Anders would be up by now. She could ask how it was going with Liesel, and tell him…

what? That she loved him? Did she still love him? She did. Did she love him enough? She had always loved him too much.

She sat up, tossing the bedcovers off, and looked at the phone on the floor near the bed. But as she reached for the receiver, she heard a voice. It was coming from the living room. She climbed out of bed and tiptoed to the door, carefully opening it and poking her head through just enough that she glimpsed the back of her father's wingback chair, the pate of his scalp shining beneath the dim glow of the reading light. She heard his voice. He laughed softly.

"It's a nice place, I suppose," he said. "I haven't decided I'll go. Eva worries. I don't want to worry her." he said. "What about you?"

Eva waited.

"Ah, I'm so sorry," he said.

She tiptoed back to the phone and, ever so softly, lifted the receiver and put it to her ear.

It was Maman! Going on in that buoyant tone of hers about the terrible cold she had over the winter, how crowded Vienna got in summer. Eva crouched against the bed, shook her head, smiling.

"I still get the Met Opera on Sundays," he said. "Last week it was *The Tales of Hoffmann*. The Domingo recording. One of my favorites."

Maman's voice warbled softly in that way she had with it, even now in her eighties. Eva listened, careful of how she breathed, remembering how Maman had taught her about the branching pathways and spaces where breath and body made a voice.

"Eva? Oh, wonderful, she's been just wonderful."

Eva placed the receiver back and leaned against the wall, eyes closed. What was this? Over the years, there'd been the occasional phone call, but nothing like this.

She slipped back into bed, resting her head on her folded arms, and drifted into sleep in the humid coolness of her room, promising herself she would call Anders later in the morning. He could tell her about Liesel, and they could talk. About so many things—the days ahead, all the years now gathered between them; a collection of days like a cycle of songs. Leaving *home* here. Returning *home* there. The fathomless ocean in between. She glimpsed it from her window seat as the plane rose into the air, how it appeared to grow larger, then smaller all at once. A skin of rippling blues and grays.

She touched her left breast, where Anders always liked resting a hand when he held her.

Sometimes, it felt as if a small fish was swimming through the chambers of her heart, sometimes a bird's fluttering wings.

A Bowl Full of Oranges

All Jozef Bastin has ever stolen are the oranges. At the age of seventy-nine, Jozef's sense of purpose has become eclipsed by a singular hunger he doesn't understand.

He reaches down, lightly running his fingers over two oranges. He eases his green mesh shopping bag around so it's near his shin and, with a little tap, the oranges topple down into the bag. Mrs. Kim doesn't notice. She's talking with Mrs. Oliver. She has already rung up his purchase of a wedge of Gouda, a quarter pound of salami, a few tomatoes and straw-berries. They've exchanged their usual pleasantries and, as is his habit, he tipped his hat politely. Mrs. Kim is always smiling and talking. She keeps her two skinny, black-haired sons busy hoisting crates of produce out into the morning sun. Some-times, when she's ringing up his purchases, she slips a head of garlic into his bag without charging him, reminding him that it's good for a pot of soup. He thanks her, looking down at the worn tops of his shoes.

Back at his apartment, he puts everything carefully away while softly humming the tune of a folksong like those his mother often sang when he was a boy. He places the oranges in a large white bowl, adding them to others taken from previous trips. He never gets around to eating them. Instead, he offers them to his neighbors or their children. His son, Nick, likes them. He winces when he sees one or two of them become mottled with that pearl gray tinge of mold before he is able to give them away and he has to throw them out. Yet, even after taking the garbage pail to the dumpster, the smell of the overripe fruit still lingers in his apartment for days.

The ripeness is a smell he loves, but at times it also repulses him.

The compulsion persists; the mound of oranges grows. Jozef is increasingly haunted by this urge, by the stirring alertness of his mind and the stillness of his heart as, week after week, he slips one or two more oranges into his bag. He marvels at how easily he takes them.

**

Saturday morning, Jozef sits at the large window in the living room of his apartment waiting for Nick. They are going to Woodlawn where Jozef's wife, Helena, is buried. Tomorrow is her birthday, and he holds in his lap a bouquet of irises, lilies of the valley, and white roses to place on her grave. He has done this faithfully every year since her death. This morning he rose early, had his coffee and a slice of buttered rye. He bathed and shaved, combed his wisps of white hair, donned a white shirt fresh from the laundry box, a dark blue blazer, gray wool slacks, and a bright red tie.

Jozef rents a four-room apartment in a red brick building four stories up on Allerton Avenue. The grounds have green lawns and tall, slender trees that make a pleasant shade.

The window lets in lots of sun, which he likes. The velvet ruby-colored sofa—a wedding gift from his mother-in-law—still endures. A threadbare oriental carpet he purchased at a flea market runs beneath. He fastidiously sweeps it each day

with a broom of stiff straw. There are a couple of low bookcases of dark wood holding a collection of art books: Modigliani,
Brancusi, Picasso, and others. They are Helena's. She was a
painter. Dear Helena, gone almost ten years now, following
years of visits to Bellevue, regimens of psychotropic drugs, a
weakened heart that finally claimed her.

Two small canvases of her work sit propped atop one book-
case: one a still-life of dishes and fruit and utensils, the other
a spare painting of glossy-leaved shrubbery and a gray-blue
sea, a tapering horizon of deep blue and mauve. Above these,
in a thin black frame, hangs an old black and white map of
Antwerp, where Jozef was born.

A small window near the bookcases holds a new air conditioner Nick got for him last summer. He rarely uses it. He
dislikes the drafty cold spots it makes.

In the corner between the bookcases and the air conditioner stands the mannequin of a male torso he once used for
fittings during his years as a shirtmaker. Its headless, mus-
lin-seamed body remains watermarked and frayed, riddled
with pinpricks and black marks of charcoal from decades of
fittings.

Jozef taps a sepia-tinged fingernail against the newspaper
wrapped around the bouquet and turns to look at the bowl
of oranges on the oval dining table. The white bowl, the dark
teak wood of the table, the vibrant color of the oranges, all
glow brightly in the light of morning. An arrangement that
might have caught Helena's eye, he thinks.

The door clicks, the knob turns. Nick. Jozef closes his eyes
as his son opens the door.

"Pop? You there? It's me."

He can smell Nick's cologne. It reeks of the oily musk of
some animal. Nick is in his mid-thirties, an investment broker
on Wall Street. He's got the necessary instincts and cunning.
He dresses in expensive clothes, has his hair cut at a salon
instead of a barbershop, dons silk socks in colors of pale blue

and yellow and shoes of exquisite nutmeg-colored Italian leather. He is tall, with shoulders bulked out, clean large hands cuffed perfectly at the wrists, nails clipped trim, square and smooth. Nick fills a room with his presence, his fine clothes, his smooth, olive skin, that spare trace of fragrant talc on the neck.

"You okay, Pop? Ready to go?"

"I'm fine." He waves his hand in the direction of his son.

Jozef sees that Nick is wearing gold cufflinks. He puts his hands on his knees, slowly rising from his chair, nodding.

"Let's go," he says as Nick helps him up, lightly brushing stray flakes of dandruff from his father's shoulders.

They take the elevator down and Nick keeps a hand on his father's elbow, gently guiding him into the passenger seat of his shiny black Lexus. Jozef watches his son, the careful way he takes his arm and helps him get into the seat, one leg at a time; the way he leans gently above him to secure his seatbelt. He is appreciative of his son's attention. It is the excess polish of Nick's life that annoys him.

He settles in, clutching the flowers in his gnarled hand.

"How much you got left to pay on this thing?"

Nick buckles himself in, turns the key in the ignition. "This beauty?" He laughs. "I don't buy, Pop. I lease. I don't like to keep a car for more than a couple of years. You know, so I lease. It's like I always have something new to drive."

That's Nick. He loves the newly minted. Anything begins to show wear, he loses interest. When Nick was a boy, he loved to run his hands over things, whether it was brass and steel tools at the hardware store, the gleam of apples and plums and packaged beef at the grocer, or the touch of cotton and silk from which Jozef fashioned shirts for his upscale clients. He delighted in helping his father pick fabrics for his shirts. He handled things with the kind of care most boys his age wouldn't dream of doing.

He hears a sound, like the chirping of an insect, and Nick reaches into his coat pocket, takes out his cell phone.

"Yeah, what's up?" he says. He nervously rubs his forehead. "Yeah...I know. Look, I can't talk right now. Can I call you later? Yeah...he's gonna be pissed, I know. So what. So he'll be pissed. I gotta go." He slips the phone back into his pocket.

"Who's pissed, Nick?"

Nick shakes his head, smirks. "It's nothing, Pop. Just the office."

On a Saturday? It's always like this when Nick visits. Vapid conversation interrupted by calls from a working life he can't seem to break away from, ever.

Jozef leans his head back against the deep cushion of his seat. The inside of the car is a hushed chamber. Noises from the street grow distant. Everything smells starkly new—the leather, the shining dashboard, the lingering drift of his son's cologne. The windshield is so clean it has vanished. The warm sun burnishes the interior.

"It's nice you can afford such a car," he says as Nick slips into reverse, cuts the wheels sharply, pulling away from the curb through bouncing glints of sun and shade, then out into the street.

**

Jozef kneels at the granite headstone and gently nestles his bouquet against it. Nick leans, kisses his fingers and touches them to the stone of his mother's grave. Jozef can feel his son's restlessness when Nick puts a hand lightly on his back and says he is going for a walk.

Jozef rests a palm against the headstone, tracing a finger along the grooved letters that spell *Helena*. A touch that awakens memory. The classroom at NYU in summer, where he came two evenings a week to take instructions in drawing—a lonely young man tired from his long days in his workroom, yet still restless. There she was, a slender young woman instructing the class, wearing khaki work pants and a white blouse over which she'd slip a paint-stained butcher's apron. Eyes large and quiet, intelligent and probing. A sheen of ethereal joy. She runs a tea-stained index finger across a square of charcoal paper, tracing the invisible curve of a line only she could see. Then she places her hand around his, guiding it until the piece of charcoal he holds makes the line—a beautiful outline of hip, thigh and leg. To be near her was to feel the glowing heat of embers.

In a city full of immigrant strangers like him, Helena became his touchstone; her hands, her voice, her laughter his map. On Sundays they would go to the Metropolitan Museum. She would dress in a dark wool skirt and a silk blouse—not for him, she would tease, but for the paintings. He couldn't yet see the affliction that was the shadow life she carried within her. His mother would have called him naïve; his father would have called him a fool. It hardly mattered. The solitary harshness of his life in the city—a raucous, money-grubbing, multi-lingual circus of concrete and steel, dense with bodies—receded in her presence, becoming a world of small and beautiful particulars: the colors of a painter's palette, eating slices of pears and oranges while sitting on a bench in Central Park beneath dappled shade as Helena spoke, in a low whisper, about Cezanne's apples. What else was life but this?

He gave her a silver ring with a diamond as small as a glint of melting ice. They were married in wintertime. Forty-five years ago, they climbed the steps of City Hall, freezing fingers entwined. A year and a half into their marriage, the manic episodes began. By then, Jozef understood that sheen in her eyes as a signal. But he was also too deeply in love. He still believed in its miracles. He became her map—calming her, coaxing her to take her lithium. She blossomed in his care.

When Helena was happy, the whole world was incandescent.

But after Nick was born, things changed. Jozef felt it coming all during her pregnancy. He saw it in the subtle ways her face flickered, as if she were moving between shadow and light and back again. She held her new baby boy as if he were a strange, delicate object. Then, she began to go days without sleep, painting and drawing, begging him to read poems to her out loud, as from the next room in their tiny apartment on East Broadway, their new baby son wailed.

One pre-dawn morning he reached for her across the bed but she wasn't there. He found her, leaning out their living room window, arms beating at some invisible thing, as if she were trying to swat leaky streaks of morning light. He held her until she went still—a nervous, exhausted bird.

He leans forward now, grips the headstone, and rises, feeling lightheaded from the rush of blood. Nick continues circling the grounds, talking softly on his cell, cutting deals among the dead.

The sun is warm on his head, his shirt growing moist. He makes his way to a nearby bench and sits, loosens his tie, pulls a handkerchief out of his back pocket, wipes his wet face.

He feels a hand on his shoulder.

"You alright, Pop?"

Jozef shrugs. "Tired. Sun's a little bright for me."

Nick sits beside his father. Jozef looks at him. His face is tight, his smile a strained muscle. His phone chirps again. Nick reaches into his pocket, swipes at the phone's screen, rises, talking softly.

"Christ," Jozef hears him mutter.

A moment later he returns to the bench, leans back, crossing his legs, his hands clasped tightly, one making a fist inside the other.

"What's wrong, Nick?"

Nick sighs. He shakes his head. "Trouble," he says.

The bench is situated on a gravel path near a small garden. Low mounds of leafy green plants fringed with bright purple and pink flowers pulse with color.

"What kind?"

Nick's face is bunched into a dark grimace. He sighs. "They've started some kind of investigation. It involves our whole firm. Insider stuff with securities, they say. I can't talk about it. Per my lawyer."

"What did you do?"

Nick shoots his father a dark, hurtful glance, then abruptly stands, hands thrust in his pockets.

"You ready to go?"

"What for?" Jozef says. "You don't like it here? You haven't even spent two minutes not being on the phone, wishing you were someplace else." Jozef's body stiffens. "Yes. Take me home," he says as he tries to stand. He grips the edge of the bench, his body lurching forward.

Nick takes his arm. "Easy, Pop, easy."

"So, they gonna let you keep your pocket phone in jail?"

"Jesus, Pop." Nick laughs. "No one's taking me to jail. I swear."

Jozef's legs feel too heavy. He breathes air into his lungs, but it only makes his body feel as if he can't get enough air. He can hardly bear it when Nick grips his elbow and escorts him to the car, explaining to his father that he has a good lawyer and he fully expects things to turn out okay.

No chance of jail for him, he says. No chance.

✳✳

Jozef feels as if he is gliding on the surface of the air, all the darkness beneath him, sunshine spilling through the shadows of trees along the parkway. The lush beauty of spring fills his lungs until his chest hurts.

Nick pulls up in front of the apartment. "You want some lunch, Pop? I could get you something from the deli."

"I'm not hungry, thanks. I'm gonna lie down."

Nick shrugs, nodding as he drums his palms against his thighs, fingers dancing. He's taken off his jacket and tossed it in the back seat and, sitting here now in his white shirt, the

58

sun glinting off his gold cufflinks, his dark trousers still bearing their fine crease, Jozef glimpses a well-groomed, middle-aged man—nervous and trying to hide it.

"Okay," Nick says. "Let's get you upstairs."

Jozef wants to say no, that he can manage on his own, that he can make it okay on his own. But he can't. It's too warm, he's too tired. Gravity, he thinks. Too much gravity in the legs.

Nick takes his key and unlocks the door, leading his father inside. The apartment is warm and dim. Jozef flips on the light switch near the door.

"Jeez, it's hot in here," Nick says, fingering the rim of his collar. "How about we switch on the air conditioner?"

"I keep it off when I'm gone. Why run up the bills?"

"It's alright, Pop. You don't have to worry. Run the thing. Keep the place cool. That's why I got it for you."

"It gets too cold in here when I run it all day."

Nick sighs, shaking his head. He goes to the air conditioner and punches the ON switch. He pulls out a dining room chair, drapes his jacket on the back, and sits.

Jozef starts for the kitchen. "You want something? A drink of water?"

"No thanks. Come sit down. Why don't you let me fix you something to eat? Maybe a sandwich?"

Jozef raises a hand in the air, shakes his head. "Stop. I'm not hungry."

He pulls out a chair across from Nick and sits. So often these days, Jozef feels that he is just close enough to Nick to sense how much distance there is between them. It isn't because Nick doesn't try. He does. He tries to be a good son. But it's what Jozef doesn't know about his life, so many things he doesn't understand.

"You remember your Uncle Theo?" Jozef asks him.

Nick cracks a smile, nods. "Yeah. I haven't talked to him in ages. You ever hear from him?"

"Oh, I get a Christmas card. Not every year, but usually," says Jozef.

"He still in Long Island?"

"Yeah. Still there. Same house."

Nick looks down. Jozef can see him nervously twirling his thumbs.

"You remember the summer you spent with him?" Jozef says.

Nick was fourteen. Jozef had sent him to stay with his Uncle Theo, Helena's brother.

"Yeah, Pop, I do." He looks at Jozef, his face quiet and even. "That was the summer Mom really went off the rails."

Helena had become prone to violent fits. Her doctors were experimenting with her medication dosages. Theo had offered to look after Nick so Jozef could take care of Helena.

"I thought your summer would be better."

"He took me to eat prime rib. A place called Chic's. It was his favorite place." Nick laughs, patting his stomach. "I ate a lot of meat that summer."

"You came back with some silver cufflinks. You've liked wearing cufflinks ever since," Jozef says.

Nick nods, smiling. "He let me pick them out myself."

It's growing cooler in the small apartment. The air conditioner hums.

"Nick?"

"Yeah, Pop?"

"You don't like visiting your mother's grave, do you."

Nick takes an orange from the white bowl, cradles it in his hand. "I don't know, Pop. It's not that, it's just...well..." He shrugs.

"Well, what?"

"Except for early on, when I was little, I can't remember a lot about her that sticks with me, except as somebody who was sick. You know?"

Jozef frowns, nods. "Yeah. Sure," he whispers.

Nick stares at the orange in his hand. "Why you buying so many of these, Pop? You on a binge?"

There's a tone of irritation in Nick's voice. He digs a big thumb into the skin and peels it back, dropping thick clumps on the table, separating the juicy segments, popping two at a time in his mouth as juice runs down his fingers. His face is moist with sweat as he grabs a white handkerchief from his back pocket, wiping his fingers.

"I give them away," says Jozef. "You like them. Where's the harm?"

Nick shrugs, smiling. He tears another segment loose and eats it. Strings of white pulp dangle from the corner of his lips. "No waste, no harm, I guess," he says, dabbing at his mouth, wiping his chin. Looking at his son devouring the orange, Jozef is reminded how his manners often fail to match the way he dresses.

"Smells like some of them might be going too ripe, you know?" says Nick. He taps his foot, the shiny leather of his shoes channeling waves of—what? Panic?

"So," Jozef says. "You got good lawyers?"

Nick looks at his father. His mouth is a tight line again, his chin stretched out hard, smooth. "I've got good lawyers. They've done lots of this stuff before. It's the usual thing. One person messes up the works for the whole firm."

"Who's messing things up?"

Nick looks at him. He rolls his lips, biting them. He shakes his head. "They have their ideas. I can't tell you anything. Please don't ask."

"Nick?"

"Pop, please..."

"Just tell me one thing. Did *you* do something wrong?"

Nick flinches, rubs his eyes wearily with the heel of his palm. "I didn't, Pop. I didn't." He looks down at the table, fingering pieces of orange peel.

Jozef looks at him, nodding. "Sure. Okay then," he says softly. "I hope it goes okay for you."

He busies himself, gathering pieces of orange peel when

Nick's phone goes off again. He starts to reach for it but Jozef grabs his wrist, squeezes it with as much strength as he's able to muster. "Don't do that," he says, a spasm of anger creeping up his spine, bone by bone.

"Huh?" Nick looks at him, startled.

"Turn that damn thing off. Quit it, will you?"

The phone continues to chirp, chirp, chirp, but Nick doesn't touch it. "Okay, okay," he says. "Sorry."

The noise stops, the apartment is quiet again.

"Can you go now?" Jozef says. "I want to lie down."

Nick's face wrinkles painfully at the sound of his father's words. He gets up, pushes the chair back against the table.

"Give me those," Nick says softly. Jozef is gathering orange peels Nick left on the table. He hands them to Nick and Nick starts for the kitchen, then stops near the trash bin, holding the peels to his nose. "I once smelled an orange from a block away. Like someone wearing too much perfume," he says, a wry smile lifting the corners of his lips. He tosses the peels in the bin.

He looks like a boy again, Jozef thinks. A hungry boy.

Jozef's palms smell of oranges too.

"I'll call you later, Pop," Nick says, returning from the kitchen where he grabs his jacket from the back of the chair, slipping his arms through the sleeves, smoothing and straightening his cuffs. He leans and puts his arms around his father, kisses his forehead.

"You need anything?"

"Like what?"

"I dunno. You need some money? Or groceries, or something?"

Jozef waves a hand at him. "Don't be silly. I'm okay. I can still get my own groceries. And I don't need your money either." His face reddens and a sudden shame engulfs him.

"Alright, alright. Be that way," Nick says. "I gotta go. Do me a favor and eat something later, will you? Promise?"

Jozef closes his eyes, raises a hand in the air. "I will."

Nick starts to leave when Jozef calls out to him.

"Nick?"

"Yeah, Pop?"

"Will you do me a favor?"

"Sure. What?"

"Next time we go to your mother's grave, bring flowers, will you?"

Nick smiles, embarrassed. "Sorry. I've been a little distracted. Next time, I promise."

As Nick shuts the door behind him, Jozef rises, heads to his bedroom. On the way, he shuts off the air conditioner. He strips down to his T-shirt, beltless slacks, bare feet, and climbs into his bed.

**

He feels it in his body, beneath layers of blankets. It is like a paralysis with interludes of near awakening and, when Jozef tries to move, his limbs won't yield. He feels damp, almost feverish. Oh, again, the lingering weight of those images. They flicker and pulse like a second heartbeat from somewhere deep inside him.

Helena's hand opens, an orange nestled in her palm, and she is whispering but he cannot hear her. Where are those tangles of threads in his brain that hold the memory of her voice?

Smoke fills the air; crates of Mrs. Kim's oranges, berries, lettuce, and cucumbers tumble and crash everywhere. Then a voice that has never faded—that of his father, the diamond cutter: *You have to hold it just so, at just the right angle. You get the right cut, you break it just right, you'll make a handful of brilliant sunshine.*

A handful of brilliant sunshine. His father had a way of holding a long concentration before making the cut.

A diamond's an ugly thing, a misshapen crystal, see? Just a piece of broken glass, until the right cut and polish turns it into a gem.

But it was Jozef, a young man in his father's dim and musty workroom in the basement of their house in Antwerp, there with Nick; not Jozef as failed lapidary, but Jozef as something of a master, speaking these words. He helps Nick clamp the diamond in the dop, helps him position it against the whirling disc, explaining the importance of the position, so the wheel grinds away the diamond to the desired angle. Nick stands on a milk stool, a small boy. Jozef wears an apron, shiny with grime and oil, one small lamp between them, burning its light down into the dop, the crystal still a roughly-shaped rock. The smells of his father's tobacco, his shaving cologne; the smells of other women, his soiled fingernails, his fine and careful hands. Between the unspoken pauses in his father's adulterous life, between the careful instructions of cleaving, day in and day out, the bombings began. The bombs whistling and shrieking like a dissonant orchestra. His father worked, disappeared, returned from his trysts like a man newly anointed with purpose. His father, always a man of purpose and poise who would never desert his family, who would suffer no betrayal of perfection honing a piece of ugly crystal into shimmering light, like someone shaping a secret.

And his mother, washing clothes by hand, boiling potatoes, counting rations, combing her long, dark hair in the evening by a light so thin her tired eyes ached and burned as she untangled her thick strands, fashioning a plump braid that ran the length of her spine; her always beautiful posture. She threads a needle and Jozef watches it disappear beneath a swath of fabric, a bobbing silver line. The tips of her fingers are pricked, bruised and dancing. His fingertips are like his mother's as he pulls thread from a large spool, unrolls bolts of fabric, shapes an arm, shapes the circumferences of collar and cuff.

One day his father goes away and never returns. Jozef

holds the memory of an enigmatic smile on his father's face as he nodded goodbye. But no, he would not say where he was off to. Passports in his mother's trembling hands, the shuffling of a large suitcase, its handle broken; burned-out churches, that empty wooden fruit cart, so familiar Jozef could find it with his eyes closed, charred and tilted at a freakish angle; empty, ransacked homes and an unsettling silence. Then he sees Nick again, steadying himself, saying he's ready to make the cut, biting his lip, wiping his hands on his shirt.

Jozef opens his eyes. He throws the blankets off, sits up, wincing; raw hunger and an ache in his temples. He grips the edge of the nightstand and rises, shoving his feet into worn leather slippers.

He fumbles through the dim living room, switches the air conditioner on. He sets it on low, resting his palm against it for a moment as it lets out a gust of cool air.

He goes to the dining room table, pulls out a chair, and sits. He takes an orange, holds it to his nose, sniffs that familiar ripeness. The fruit is still good, not yet too far gone. He digs a thumbnail into the skin, begins to peel the orange. The tips of his fingers are fragrant with the smell, the snowy, musty pulp. Carefully, he separates the sections and one by one, slips them into his mouth, closing his eyes as he chews, tears sliding down his cheeks, seeds slipping out between his lips, into his palm tightly cupped beneath his chin, the sweet juice filling tongue and cheek, his hunger expanding as the fruit disappears, encroaching the last unlit place of his days.

The White Cliffs Hotel

Could it really be, what, over fifty years?

At the curved portal leading to the dining room, the familiarity of the hotel floated before him in fragments. The tall white columns at the entrance looked more slender. The veranda was now enclosed by glass. The apron of well-manicured lawn, as deeply green as malachite, was still there, and so was the seafront balcony. The terrace was still flanked by large black urns, and this morning they were full of red geraniums fading with the dying of summer. The dining room was smaller than he remembered, but it still had those same arched windows that ran from floor to ceiling. They were no longer adorned with the long green velvet curtains. The wood floors in the corridors still creaked beneath worn Turkish runners.

He had taken the train from Cambridge, a trail of gold and russet leaves and the autumn sky seeming to follow him all the way here. He awoke in the dark morning, his body still jet-lagged from the long trip across the Atlantic three days earlier. His old legs, the intractable, unforgiving aches from muscles and joints, urged him out of bed. A bed that felt as unsettling, as inevitable as the grave itself. There wasn't, after all, much left of the unused portion of his life.

A little later, showered and shaved and dressed, he waited for pale light to emerge, impatient with the gnawing of his stomach. He sat by the window, his ebony cane between his legs, fingering the beribboned medal Cambridge had posthumously bestowed to his father which he had been called upon to collect in his honor. How his father might be so much more pleased with this medal than with his son. It would have offered a bittersweet vindication.

**

The dining room was almost deserted save for a young couple with a baby. It was autumn, after all. They sat beneath an ancient dust-cloaked chandelier in the center of the room, the woman feeding the baby as her husband studied a map. This hotel was an in-between place—not as much a destination as an interlude—where you consulted your map, seeking to chart a journey along those shores where England met the Strait of Dover looking across to France.

Through his tottering, watery-eyed vision, this couple and their child, sitting among all the other vacant cloth-covered tables, looked at once self-contained and somewhat misplaced. Against the wall near the kitchen loomed another figure: a teenage boy, resting in between his rounds of sweeping and mopping, sat in a soiled apron reading the newspaper and drinking a canned soda.

He moved cautiously, gripping his cane, trying to adjust his faltering vision against the lengthening morning light. He chose a table in the corner, close to a window that gave him a view of the sea. The tablecloth was freshly pressed. He fingered the line of its hem. How pleasant it felt, as if someone still cared that it should be so. Even with the windows closed he could smell the thick, salty air. The sun was rising higher, making the room brighter, warmer, though not enough to release the chill in his bones. In sharp, telegraphic waves, he suddenly glimpsed at once an image of his younger self and the old man he had become. He felt his heart falter a little, as it often did these days. There was almost no one left from his younger days. The present world was more like a dream to him than what had once been real in his life. His wife of forty years was gone, dead going on three summers. He had stopped loving her after twenty years, a testament not only to his strident honesty but also a deeper shame he had failed to reconcile. This quiet betrayal of heart and spirit had lodged itself permanently inside him, as densely intertwined as a tumor in a thicket of nerves. And there were his two grown sons in separate states who only occasionally kept in touch. They had not yet desired to give him any grandchildren.

He had come to this hotel with his parents during a summer between the wars. They were returning to America, his father having completed his scholarly sojourn in archaeology at Cambridge. He was just a teenager then, and he dreaded returning to an America that would be so much stranger to him than when they'd left years earlier, with him just a couple of years from finishing elementary school. He was certain that further alienating cruelties awaited him. It was like that every time they moved.

Now, he could see that familiar white stone terrace and, beyond it, the tide-worn pebbles of the shore and the gray sea lifting itself. The first time he saw the girl was from that terrace. He was having breakfast with his parents. His father read out loud the timetables for taking the ferry to Calais while his mother, wearing a wide-brim straw hat, stirred her tea.

He had seen the girl when he turned to look off in the distance. Such was his habit whenever his parents engaged in their dull conversations. The girl had been walking alone along the shore. His heart had quickened at the sight of her, the ease with which she strolled, drinking in the morning as if it were hers and hers alone. Now and then she would stop to collect shells within the upturned dome of her straw hat. She knelt and touched the shore with a kind of patient, unconscious freedom. She wore a black bathing suit, her body as pale as the talcum his mother would put on her arms and neck in summer. He remembered her dark hair, wet against her skin.

The waiter appeared with a pot of tea. He was tall and thin, his face riddled with lines, his complexion brown and ruddy. He wore a white shirt, its cloth so threadbare the flesh of his chest could be glimpsed through its sheen. His collar was loose, showing the gaunt extremes of his neck as hollow as a shadowy cave. He exuded a ghostly loneliness as he slid the small vase of white carnations to the corner of the table, setting the pot down, carefully placing cream and sugar alongside.

"Toast?"

"Of course," he said, nodding.

"Eggs?"

"Two. Poached lightly. Thank you."

"Name and room number?"

"Brightman. Room 210."

"Come to see the cliffs, have you, Mr. Brightman?" The waiter smiled. His hands were behind his back and he stood as if drawn to the light from the window.

"Well, yes, sure," he said, nodding as if to convince himself. "Really the main thing to see here."

The waiter nodded slowly, pursing his lips.

"What part of America are you from?"

"Detroit. Michigan."

"Ah! Where they make, or should I say, once made the automobiles?"

Mr. Brightman nodded. "Difficult days," he said.

The waiter turned Mr. Brightman's cup upright and poured tea.

"They'll pass, no doubt," he said, carefully setting the pot back down.

Mr. Brightman smiled politely, nodding.

"It's quite pleasant here," continued the waiter. "Even in October. Bit more deserted though." He looked down at his guest, still smiling, but with the distracted air of polite indifference. A rod of sunlight touched his ear. He tilted his head away from the warmth. He didn't seem to be in any hurry.

"The cliffs are nice," he continued. "But I must confess I'm afraid they don't really interest me much. Perhaps because I live here."

"Actually, I was here many years ago. As a teenager. I'm really surprised to discover the hotel is still here."

"Ah," the waiter said, "a nostalgic pilgrimage."

"Well, I suppose," said Mr. Brightman, stirring his tea, feeling self-conscious as he lifted the cup to his lips.

"Place was really quite damaged during the war. Lots of refurbishing had to be done."

Mr. Brightman nodded. He waved a withered hand in the air. "Oh yes, I remember. Though we'd been here before the bombings. I thought about it a lot back home when the war broke out. I was young, but I remember."

"I was just a lad meself," said the waiter. "Our family lived in Folkestone, southwest of here. Terrible days." He frowned, shrugging. "You would see the strangest things. Whole cottages blown wide open." He made a sweeping gesture with his hands. "But a bedroom on the second floor might be left standing, the bed still there, some poor soul lying in it rubbing his eyes, wondering what in bloody hell happened." He laughed, showing his bad teeth. His eyes had a sudden shining exuberance. His skin flushed bright pink.

"Incredible," Mr. Brightman said, shaking his head. "I remember the newsreels." He sat in the dark movie house watching the shining world going up in flames, his heart racing. Afterward, he'd step out into the raw bleached light of endlessly peaceful days, riding his bicycle as if he were trying to outrun both boredom and calamity.

"The castle alone would be worth the climb. It's really quite interesting."

Mr. Brightman blinked, nudged back to the present by the waiter's voice. "The climb?" He smiled. "I'm sorry, I didn't get what you were saying."

"You know, the castle. Dover Castle. It sits atop the cliffs." He made a climbing motion with his fingers. "Lots of people like to hike up the cliffs to the castle."

Mr. Brightman nodded. The castle. Of course. How could he forget? His heart lurched. The girl had taken him by the hand, leading him up the path, through the thick trees, the leaves like outstretched hands, light spilling around them.

He patted his hand against his cane on the back of his chair, shaking his head. "I'm afraid I don't do much climbing these days." He chuckled.

"Oh well, if you don't wish to climb, you needn't worry," said the waiter. "Our concierge sells passes, a nice little package. Air-conditioned bus, a snack, a complete guided tour, your own little souvenir booklet that gives you the whole history in a nutshell. And they've got audio tapes too, old recordings of Churchill urging everyone to keep some spine. Quite a worthwhile bang for your buck, I'd say."

"Really," Mr. Brightman said, half-curious, half-distracted by the sudden drift of memories. Her voice, clear and light, had turned suddenly to a throaty whisper the further they'd climbed, the deeper into the trees they'd gone, as if trying to escape the penetrating sunlight. She had gripped his hand so tightly. They'd found a leafy shelter from where they could see the lip of horizon and sea.

"You can tour the secret tunnels."

Mr. Brightman paused, his face lighting with recognition at the sound of these words. "Ah, yes!" he said. "Where they evacuated the troops from Dunkirk?"

"Headquarters of Operation Dynamo," the waiter said, "hundreds of thousands strong. All working like a well-oiled machine." He shook his head. "Those were the days." His sigh hung in the air like a stale breeze. The pink had faded from his skin, his flesh pale and slack again.

The men grew quiet, overtaken by a sudden shyness. Mr. Brightman's stomach grumbled again and, embarrassed, he covered it with a hand.

"So," the waiter finally spoke, "poached eggs and toast. I'll have it out shortly." He turned and walked away.

The baby wailed softly from across the dining room. The mother crooned, tapping her spoon against a bowl of warm cereal. The father sipped his tea, still absorbed in his map reading.

Minutes later, the waiter returned with Mr. Brightman's breakfast, setting the plate carefully in front of him, politely imploring him to enjoy. He stood there as Mr. Brightman took his knife and fork in hand.

"Yes, yes," the waiter said, almost in a whisper. "These days, the best reason to come here is to watch the young women in summer." As he spoke, he motioned with his head toward the window, his eyebrows dancing up and down. "Right out there on the terrace, sitting in the sun in their bikinis. Wonderful, it is. Some days are just absolutely wonderful when the sun is high in the sky and the terrace is full of women." His skin flushed warmly again.

Mr. Brightman looked at the waiter, a little shocked by the sound of such pure desire entwined with anticipation. He seemed like a predatory fish, the way he breathed through his nose, nostrils flaring like gills. He kept his hands behind his back, rocking softly on his heels as if waiting to be swept away by some beautiful mermaid.

Mr. Brightman stirred his tea, smeared chilled butter and marmalade on his toast.

"By the way, if you're interested in the guided tour, I can let the concierge know," said the waiter.

Mr. Brightman smiled, dabbing toast crumbs from his lips

with his napkin. He felt suddenly drained and couldn't fathom the thought of Churchill's voice droning in his ear as a tour guide walked them among the propped and straightened rubble of the past.

"Oh, not today. Perhaps another time, thank you."

The waiter gave a slight bow, nodding in Mr. Brightman's direction, and began to busy himself, moving among the empty tables, smoothing the tablecloths, centering the bud vases, straightening chairs.

Mr. Brightman took a bite of toast, sipped his tea, salted his eggs. He looked out the window, still feeling the waiter's movements between tables, his vigilant outward gaze. The child cooed softly now, his mother gently coaxing with pleasing phrases as if she were embroidering a whole universe, carefully, with needle and thread.

He closed his eyes for a few brief seconds, then swallowed.

All those years ago, the girl had led him through shadow and dappled sun to a place of cool stone and grass amid the shelter of tall trees. They laughed, spilling the shells from her hat. She picked one up and held it in her palm, running her finger over it. "A tiny thing," he remembered her saying, "all hollowed out and worn by the sea. That's what I like best about it." Then he heard his father's voice, down below on the shore, calling out his name. He had pretended not to know him, saying to her he must be some kind of madman. He spread his hand out before her and she traced his lifeline with her finger, telling him he would live a long time, and then she pressed the worn shell in his palm. His fingers grazed hers. His father shouted his name again, only this time it made her stiffly sit up as if overcome by a quickening panic. She stood, gathered her hat and the shells, muttering something about how she had to go, and before he could do or say anything, she was gone. She had left him there, awakened, aroused, and alone. For the first time in his life, he had wondered what would become of him in this world.

Now, there was no one on the shore, no one on the terrace, and no one this early in the morning would be climbing the path to the castle grounds. But Mr. Brightman smiled, remembering the girl, how she placed that shell in his hands, the warm feel of her fingers touching his. They were nothing more than a couple of fumbling adolescents. They hadn't even properly introduced themselves. In his haste to rise and start after her, he had dropped the shell; she was gone, and the moment dissolved into awkward humility, then worldly wonder, before he felt again that familiar confusion and boredom.

Years later, when the course of his life had altered itself, becoming at once more purposeful and more sadly complicated, he thought the girl was someone he had only imagined. And that shell—that weathered fragment of shell that slipped from his hand—still held a strange and stinging tactile clarity.

The mother lifted her child from the highchair. The father looked up, folding his map, then held it up in front of his face— up and down and up again, peeking and hiding as the child squealed with delight.

Mr. Brightman turned and looked at the waiter, whose figure, moving among the neat lines of empty tables, occasionally eclipsed by flooding sunlight, seemed to be getting smaller. He would turn his head, looking out the window, folding napkins, lightly running his fingers along the backs of chairs, no doubt dreaming of the girls who would arrive in summer.

Needles

The needle popped up through the cloth, a trail of green embroidery thread emerging as Breanne watched her cousin Grace swiftly grasp the needle between thumb and forefinger and drive it back down and through the underside of the cloth. Up and down the needle went, bobbing and dancing—a silver stem gathering threads of color. Beneath the disc of tightly stretched cloth, Breanne glimpsed a tangle of bright threads, like wires.

All that year, time had passed achingly slowly, and Breanne had wondered if summer would ever come. Grown-ups whispered about *the fevers*, neighbors on both sides of her house and across the street all vanished from their front porches. Swimming pools, drinking fountains, and puddles of water still brought fears. She'd grown used to lying awake in the dark, her eyes adjusting so she could make out the shapes of things.

But here, out on the screened porch of Grace's parents' house, it was quiet. A different kind of silence that felt easier for both Breanne and Grace. They sat on a wicker settee, not always talking, but not feeling awkward when they didn't.

The soft, low notes of *Love Me Tender* played from a portable Zenith on a small metal table at Grace's elbow, alongside her steel crutches, leaning at a deep slant. She stopped her needlework, closed her eyes, humming softly.

All the older girls loved Elvis. Well, even *love* seemed too small a word. They went crazy nuts wild for him. Breanne figured it must have been the song making her cousin breathe like that.

She held a cardboard clown in her lap, idly fingering its legs as she listened to the lilting trail of her cousin's voice while quietly watching the way Grace worked with her hands because from Grace's hands Breanne had always seen things emerge, first quietly, then suddenly, like a burst of confetti. She could make shadow rabbits and birds that hopped and flew across the flowered wallpaper of Breanne's bedroom. A language before Breanne ever knew how to speak.

It was raining—a plentiful June rain that shimmered through the dark leaves of the magnolias, and the fullness of the trees held the rain, slowing it to an easy falling. Grace said the screened porch was the best thing about the house. Breanne liked the way she described it: a place where you could be inside and outside at the same time.

When the song was over, Grace opened her eyes, then quickly shut them again, squeezing them more tightly this time, and Breanne wondered if her cousin dreamed. Maybe of falling in love? Or would she have nightmares like Breanne did before she learned to make out shapes in the dark?

When Grace opened her eyes again, her face relaxed. She breathed more softly now. She straightened herself, twisting her upper body as she turned to switch off the radio. Breanne waited in case Grace might take her crutches to go to the kitchen for something and Breanne would need to be ready.

"Well, you look like you're either bored or afraid to talk," said Grace. "Which is it?"

Breanne felt her face grow warm. She wasn't sure what to say. Grace was right about feeling bored, but the truth made Breanne feel shy.

Grace held up her needlework in front of Breanne. "You

want to try a little embroidery?"

"Really?" Breanne said. She nodded eagerly, quickly folding the clown and letting it drop from her fingers to the floor.

"You've never done it before, have you?"

"No," said Breanne.

"It's not all that hard," Grace said. "Takes a little practice. Then you get a certain rhythm going."

Grace's voice. Clear as always. Its edges clean and tucked. But glancing down at her cousin's legs buckled in those braces, Breanne thought Grace's voice and her legs didn't go together. She wanted to ask her how it felt, but couldn't think of how to do that in any way that wouldn't sound wrong. Grace was like she'd always been, but, at the same time, she'd become someone different. She'd come back home after her first year of college on those steel crutches. And she hardly ever talked about what happened to her. No one else spoke about it either. Everybody was terrified about the polio. It wasn't something you could see. Not in the water. Not in the dirt playgrounds at school. People on Breanne's block went from sitting on their front porches after supper, letting their kids turn water hoses on the neighbor's kids, to shutting themselves away. Like they didn't exist anymore. And, after Grace returned home, Breanne hadn't been allowed to see her. *Not until you get your shot*, her mother insisted. Breanne recalled a hushed sadness in her mother's eyes when Grace's name was mentioned.

It was Grace who had taught Breanne how to swim. People used to talk about what a natural Grace was. How her body took to the water like that was where she always belonged. When Grace was eleven and Breanne just two, she would hold Breanne in the water, her hands cupping Breanne's waist, her calm voice urging Breanne to kick her legs.

The following summer, she had held Grace's hand, trembling when Grace yelled *"Jump!"* and into the pool they plunged. Beneath the water, still clasping Grace's hand, she had watched their legs floating, Grace's dark mane drifting around her like one of her mother's silk scarves, her body a twirling spear; and Breanne's body, smaller—she felt swallowed by all that blue-green water. She thought she'd disappear if she let go of Grace. But it was Grace who suddenly let go, vanishing, and for a few terrified seconds Breanne floated, kicking her small legs as Grace dove beneath her, making her body a raft around which Breanne straddled her legs and clasped her arms. Grace's arms became wings cutting the water as they surfaced.

Grace made a couple more stitches then lowered the circle of cloth so Breanne could see. There, framed by the disc, a slender branch with leaves shooting off its sides. Breanne ran an index finger over the threads in different shades of green, her mouth a hushed *o*. The threads were smooth and tight. What a wonderful thing. Something that could never come undone.

"I make my own patterns," Grace said.

"How do you do it?"

Grace took a slow breath in, then out. Breanne watched her chest rise and sensed something like a secret lodged there in the way Grace's breath filled her lungs. She looked down again at Grace's thin legs, the pale flesh jutting from her culottes; and at her feet, clad in white socks and black leather shoes with thick soles.

Grace placed two fingers beneath Breanne's chin and lifted it. Breanne looked into her eyes—the *hush* there like a curtain. She raised her embroidery hoop where Breanne could see, fluttering her fingers.

"You ready?"

Breanne nodded. When she was allowed to swim again, she would make her body a raft upon which her cousin could float and she'd carry her from one end of the pool to the other.

"Okay," Grace said, "the way I do it is, I start with one color, through the needle, and, well, I just keep going. You gather one part of a picture, then another. Bit by bit." She plunged the needle down through the cloth again, snugly pulling on it, then flipped the hoop over and ran the needle beneath a stitch and back up. She held needle and thread aloft, pulled tightly on the thread, took it between her teeth, and snipped it. She wound it around an index finger, looping and knotting it, then handed the needle to Breanne.

"First you have to learn how to thread a needle and make good knots."

Breanne nodded, took the needle between thumb and forefinger, a thin and weightless thing. As she held it, she remembered getting her polio vaccination back at the start of the school year. Everyone was getting them now. She couldn't bear the sight of the needle and had looked down at the tops of her loafers, the lace edges of her white socks, praying for it to be over.

Grace sifted through her sewing box, lifted a curled nest of maroon thread, unwinding it.

"Here, take this," she said. "And hold the needle up. See that hole? That's called the eye of the needle."

Breanne did as she said, lifting the needle to the light where she could see the hole, then took the thread and held it there, reminded of how, as she waited, the nurse had held the needle up to the fluorescent light of the ceiling, gently flicking a finger against the translucent scale.

"I wet the thread a little between my lips first," Grace said. "Makes it easier to slip it through."

Breanne ran her tongue along her lips, placed the thread between them. But as she drew the thread out, the needle slipped from her grasp.

"Oops," Grace said with a trickle of laughter. She pointed to the floor near the metal heel of one of her leg braces.

Breanne knelt and pinched it from the floor and as she tried to position the needle between her fingers for threading, she accidentally pricked the tip of her right index finger.

"Ouch."

"*Like a bee sting,*" the nurse had said. Breanne's mother had perched herself on a little stool with wheels, her nervous hands fingering the brass closure of her handbag. Then came the sting, and the shame Breanne felt when her eyes watered. She chewed the inside of her lip, determined to keep quiet. The pale green walls of the clinic clouded, blurring, the nurse's white shoes melting against Breanne's loafers.

"Roll the needle between your fingers," Grace told her. "And don't worry. You'll do that more times than you can count before you're through." She opened one of her hands, unfolding her fingers. "See?"

Breanne regarded the callused tips of Grace's fingers, the places where the needle had pierced her skin so many times over that Grace said she no longer felt pain.

"Go ahead," Grace said, her voice quiet, low yet still coaxing. "Really. Touch one of my fingers with the needle."

Breanne took the needle, lightly skating its tip across the hard flesh of Grace's right thumb.

"Oh, that's nothing. Give it a poke," said Grace.

Breanne shook her head. When the nurse finished, she had swabbed Breanne's arm again with a cotton ball soaked in alcohol. So cold on her skin, it made goosebumps. Her nose filled with the alcohol's sharp, unpleasant smell. And then her mother touched the band-aid on Breanne's arm with a finger: *"Don't forget. That little sting will spare you those leg braces."* The sound of her mother's voice different. Still weary, yes, but less nervous, and in her face, ease there too, until Breanne had asked about Grace—why hadn't she gotten the bee sting? Couldn't she get it now? Her mother shook her head while crushing the butt of her cigarette on the sidewalk with her shoe. *"Think of yourself as lucky, Breanne."*

What did her mother mean? Was Grace going to die? Could she go and see Grace now? Could she visit when summer came? Did her mother hate Grace? Was that it? Her mother ordered her to hush, gripping Breanne's shoulders as they walked from the clinic to the car, until Breanne cried out, twisting free from her.

Now Breanne still hesitated, so Grace took the needle from her and poked the tip of her thumb. She smiled. "It's okay. Really."

Breanne looked at her cousin. "I don't know…"

"Here," Grace said impatiently. She wrapped her hand around Breanne's, placed the needle again between Breanne's fingers. Next, she took the thread and measured a portion no longer than an eyelash, which she then coaxed delicately and precisely within the eye of the needle.

"Now grab on to that, go on."

With thumb and forefinger, Breanne pulled on the thread, once, then again, slowly streaming it through the needle's eye. That worked. It felt good, too. Grace wound the bottom strands of thread around Breanne's index finger and slowly Breanne struggled—once, twice, three times—to complete the knot, the threads still slipping from her fingers the harder she tried. She slumped.

"I can't get it," she said.

"Oh, nonsense," Grace said. "Make a circle and slip the tail end of the strands through it." She opened her palm, laying the threaded ends across. "Do it."

Breanne started twisting the threads again as Grace's fingers—hovering, barely touching—guided hers, and the ends found the loop, and this time Breanne got them through, and she pulled on them until the loop shrank into a knot hardly the size of a grain of sand.

"You got it. See?" said Grace.

Breanne nodded without looking up. They kept going, Grace's hands guiding Breanne's fingers. When Breanne would stick the needle through the cloth, Grace's fingers would retrieve it from beneath, pulling it down, sending it back up. And Breanne would wait, watching the needle rise before taking it again. How satisfying that felt. How surprising her pleasure. Back and forth, up and down, the dancing lightness of fingers making one stitch, then another, the needle a shimmering pulse gathering, moving, and gathering one color and then another into the emergent shape of a new branch, the beginnings of a leaf.

"That's real good, Breanne."

Breanne smiled. This was a new kind of pleasure, guiding the needle, making it do what you wanted it to do. Like the time Grace let go of her in the water, urging her forward, Breanne's legs and arms—and her heart too—fluttering like moth wings.

"You can show your momma what you learned," Grace said. "We'll start a new one for you. You can take it with you. Practice."

Breanne saw the toe of her mother's shoe, her ankle, wagging in a half circle as she crushed out that cigarette on the hot sidewalk outside the clinic, the sun on their backs. Her mother had pulled a compact mirror from her purse, studying her lips, running her pinky finger along the bottom, the corners, as if to rearrange the plum color of her mouth. She tilted the mirror up and Breanne could see that familiar weariness in her eyes reflected there, the tip of her finger running along the shadows beneath, rubbing at them as if trying to erase them. A coin of sunlight struck the mirror, making the light dance, making her mother wince.

The rain pattered softly now, like someone whispering. Warm, sweet smells lifted from the magnolia. Breanne heard her mother's voice again, whispering: *"You know, it was me who taught Grace how to swim?"* She slipped the key into the ignition, sighing, staring through the windshield at what, exactly, Breanne couldn't see. And then, she folded a hand over Breanne's and gently squeezed. *"Don't ever say anything about what I just said, Bre. You know. About Grace."*

"Think of something you'd like to make," said Grace.

Breanne tried, but felt struck with nothing more than simple, rock-heavy dumbness.

"What kinds of things do you like?"

Breanne considered trees, the sun, the colored candy from the Pez dispensers. Birds too. She hooked her thumbs together and fluttered her fingers, moving her hands up and down, making flying motions.

"Birds," she said, watching her hands. "I like birds."

She scooted forward, her arms outstretched, her hands making a faintly dancing shadow on the rough wood floor. Then Grace lifted her own hands and gently folded them over Breanne's. She turned them so Breanne's palms faced up, then hooked her thumbs.

"Like that," she said. She made a fluttering bird with her own hands as Breanne watched, seeing again the flowered wallpaper in her long-ago bedroom, the rapid flurry of Grace's hands transforming from rabbit shadow to bird shadow to floating starfish shadow.

Breanne made her bird like Grace had shown her—a bird whose wings she imagined cutting through the rain, circling back around, landing slow and light on her cousin's shoulder.

High Grass

I'm chasing after my older sister, Shelly—I'm the sheriff, she's the gold thief—when all of a sudden she stops cold in her tracks and I can tell by the stiff, vertical tilt of her body that something is wrong. I catch up to her and can hear her breathing hard. She's trying to speak but can't and before my eyes can fix on him, I hear that sound. Shelly pointed at his raised head there among the shafts of tall, dry grass. I know this is not a good sign. I could see his forked tongue slithering in and out. It looked like a thin black wire spliced at the end. Wet and coated with its poison, it is still the image I see when I think of meanness. When you're looking at a snake's tongue, you believe you're seeing an evil thing, let me tell you.

And that rattle. Jesus Christ, how that sound filled the air all around us. I couldn't believe it. If I'd wanted to say anything (I couldn't; my throat had dried up, just like Shelly's) I'm sure I wouldn't have been able to hear my own words. Like a bunch of BB gun pellets rattling inside a can right up close to your ear, that's what it was like.

I don't know what the Good Lord was thinking when he made snakes. No arms, no legs. They're like some crazed, poisonous thing in a straitjacket.

I've lost a lot of things in my lifetime. I've screwed up a

lot, too. And I'm always amazed at the things other people say I did that I can't remember. But this is one day that stays with me, one piece I haven't lost. Over forty years ago, under that unmerciful West Texas sun.

So Shelly and me, we're standing there looking at this coil of sinuous evil loaded with venom, and all of a sudden she starts nervously muttering. "Jesus oh Jesus Weldon," she says. And I'm afraid she's going to start screaming or peeing in her pants or something like that and I start to get real nervous myself.

I remember the crisp snapping of grasshoppers rubbing their legs together and from the sides of my eyes I glimpse their hopping motions in the high blades of grass. I'm sweating buckets and this has attracted a bevy of midges and gnats circling about my head eager for the wet salt of my skin. Then I feel my throat opening a bit and I whisper to Shelly to hush. She's trembling like a shrub trying to buck a high wind.

What a long moment. Standing there like that. A lot of things began to run through my mind. I wouldn't say it was one of those *your-whole-life-passes-in-front-of-you* moments, but it was pretty close. We hadn't lived long enough to know what regret was and I don't remember thinking about wishing I'd done this or that. But along with the dancing of the grasshoppers and the dizzying orbits of those gnats and midges, I began seeing the unsettling images of my miserable family. First, that of our dead mother, Lily, just dark curls and that constant woeful expression she wore. Then our father, Rupert, so drunk most of the time that the dawn of any new day usually left him feeling insulted. I could see him trying to swing a fist in the air at anyone who would take it. Then of course Uncle Will and Aunt Carla, who were only marginally suitable as our *guardians* (a term the court used, which struck me then and strikes me still as laughable). But, as Uncle Will was fond of reminding us, their obliging to take custody of us was, at best, grudging. I'm thinking if we make it back, he's likely to be pissed at our being late for supper, even if there's a good reason for it (which as far as I'm concerned there certainly is, since I believe exhibiting stillness and patience in the presence of a creature like this snake ranks right up there with the best of them). And I fully expect he'll have some sort of punishment on his mind.

Something about the rush of my thoughts that makes me feel my whole family is standing there watching me gets me riled. I don't want to die. It's not my time. And I know another thing too, feeling Shelly shaking beside me. I don't want anything to happen to her.

Something shifts inside me. I don't know what, but I just decide we're going to get out of there somehow. My mind suddenly feels clear, my thoughts focused. I don't even notice the midges and gnats anymore. My hands are balled up tight and I can feel the sweat in my palms and a pulse thumping right in their centers. My ears throb so much they hurt. But I feel calm as I look down at my feet.

I spot a rock beside my left foot. It's a good-sized one. A simple plan forms in my mind. Throw the rock, just easy enough and far enough, to distract the snake so we can get away. But I don't move yet. I'm looking at the snake, which appears to be looking straight back at us, that tongue darting and dancing. Still, if I'm going to do what I've got in mind, I've got to start making a move.

Slowly, I crouch enough so I can pick up that rock.

Shelly is still breathing fast as I close my hand around it. It's a little bigger than my palm and, having soaked up the sun all day, it's hot. I shut my eyes, count to five, and throw it off to my left and start yelling run Shelly, run now.

To this day, I've never been sure what actually happened next because one thing doesn't necessarily follow another in a moment like that. All I remember are these two things: the snake rising like a whirling dervish into the air and that Shelly is absolutely not going to move no matter what I say, even though I'm yelling like the devil himself is at our heels. I realize the rock has not landed where I intended. Instead of merely distracting the snake, I've startled the hell out of him. And I'm not at all interested in gauging his response, let me tell you.

I grab Shelly by the wrist while still yelling run, run. At first, she's like a limp rag doll and the expression on her face is a frozen mask of terror-bleached white like a Halloween ghost. Finally, she starts moving her legs and I start pumping mine and we're running so fast I feel like my lungs are going to explode. At some point, she breaks away from me and starts running even faster until she's ahead of me and I can see her in a cloud of dust, her dark hair flying behind her, the "Y" of her overalls stark against her white blouse, her sunburned arms tight against her body and swinging like pendulums.

She's moving uphill now, toward the house, and by this time the late afternoon sun is making our shadows long and deep. I finally catch up with her. As I make my way up the hill, I see her, bent at the waist, hands on her knees, head down, trying to catch her breath. I catch up to her, trying to steady my own breathing. I start spitting because it feels like my lungs are full of sand.

"Holy Moses Weldon," Shelly says. "What'd you do? What happened?"

"I threw a rock. I was trying to distract him."

She stares at me, her eyes as hard and dry as the ground we're standing on. "That was brilliant."

I can hear the sarcasm in her voice and I don't like it. I kick at the ground between us and a swirl of dry dust rises up.

"We got away, didn't we?" I say. "You just stood there ogling him like you didn't have anything better to do."

She thrusts her hands in her back pockets and toes into a cluster of dead weeds with her sneaker, shrugging.

"He sure was big," she finally says, her voice low.

"Biggest one I've ever seen," I say.

Then she looks over at the house. I turn and look too, and then we look at each other.

"Don't say anything," she says. "Not a word."

"Not me." I say, drawing a big "X" over my heart with my finger.

"Anyway, it's late and they're already gonna be mad," she says. "You know what that means."

"No supper," I say. "Fine. We'll wait 'til they're in bed, then raid the kitchen."

We quietly stare at the house. As far as we're concerned, we'd rather go just about anywhere else, and to us it is just a house—just a roof with walls, not the refuge of home. That it would take a snake's wrath to send us running toward it has to tell you something.

And then I hear her whisper: "God, I hate them. I'd rather keep a snake company."

I can't help but laugh at this, and I lift my arm in the direction from which we've just frantically fled. "Go right ahead," I say.

This gets her to laughing and I'm glad because Shelly's about the only thing I've got left in this world that hasn't turned as ugly as that snake.

We start together toward the house, and as we're walking along she suddenly pats me on the shoulder and thanks me for getting us out of there. I shrug and say you're welcome. I always feel something within me quicken when my sister actually shows kindness.

As we get closer to the house, I see that the carport—with its rusted and slanting corrugated tin roof—is empty. Uncle Will's Buick is nowhere to be seen. The shadows on the front porch are deep and speak of emptiness. There are no lights on in the house and the vinyl shades have not been raised for the evening.

"There's nobody here," I say.

"Hot dog," Shelly says, clasping her hands together. "You

know why? It's Friday. Friday is their party night. I forgot 'til now."

I remember now too. She starts running for the front porch, yelling.

"C'mon, let's go," she says. "The place is ours."

We make it to the front door and she turns the knob but nothing happens. She pushes against it. "It's locked." Jesus Christ. They've locked us out? We look at each other, our eyes wide. "Let's go 'round the back," she says and off she goes with me fast behind her. I see her starting to open the screen door, but as I'm coming up the steps she says, "Holy Moses."

"What?"

"The screen door is latched," she says. She's really mad. She kicks at it with the toe of her sneaker and it rattles. It's an old wooden door and chips of already cracked white paint come off it. Then she turns to me.

"You got your pocketknife with you?"

I reach into the back pocket of my jeans and pull it out—this one thing my father gave me when I turned five. I like it almost better than anything else I have.

"You're not gonna cut the screen, are you?"

Shelly rolls her eyes impatiently. "For crying out loud, doofus, how else you expect we're going to get in? You want to sleep in the bushes tonight?"

"He'll kill us both if he finds out," I say.

"He won't even notice," she says. I give her the knife. But I don't like this. She takes it, raises the silvered blade from its folds, places it between where the wood frame meets the screen, and starts sawing until she's made a clean L-shaped cut along that seam. She lifts up the corner, slips her wrist through, and unlatches the door. Now we're standing in the small square space between the screen door and the door that leads to the kitchen and as Shelly puts her hand on the door-knob she closes her eyes. "Please, please open," she whispers. Then she turns the knob.

We're in. The kitchen is dim and empty, slanting bars of orange sunlight running along the worn linoleum. I am suddenly so hungry I feel like I could eat half a cow. But as I look around at the stove, the small Formica dining table, the countertops, I realize there's nothing in the way of any kind of supper that's been left for us.

Shelly has stepped back toward the screen and is humming as she tucks the cut corner back into place. The next thing I know, she pulls out some bread from the bread bin, grabs a big knife from the drawer, and starts slicing. She cuts thick slices that fall one on top of the other. Then she pulls out some butter and strawberry jam from the refrigerator.

"C'mon, let's eat," she says.

We start spreading butter and jam, lots of it, on the bread. Then she puts a hand on my shoulder, pats it lightly. "Go sit down, I'll bring this to the table." I look at her. She seems so calm and suddenly so much older.

"Go on!" she says. "What're you waiting for?" I go to the table, pull out a chair and sit.

She puts the bread on a plate and sets that down in the center of the table, then goes to the refrigerator again, pulls out a jar of something, and brings that to the table.

I look at its label. "Pickles?"

"They're sweet pickles. Real good." Her eyebrows dance up and down. She pours two glasses of milk, pulls out a chair with her foot, and sits across from me.

We eat. That first bite of thick bread, sweet jam, and butter is like pure heaven. Every bone in my body is ready to sing. And then I take a swallow of cold, sweet milk and close my eyes and thank the Good Lord the snake didn't land on top of us and also for Shelly's evident skills at breaking and entering. Then I open my eyes and look over at her and I see she's also scarfing down her bread and jam and some of those sweet pickles like a rodent going after a scrap of cheese and I see her glass of milk is almost all gone.

"Why'd they lock us out like that? You think they just forgot?"

She stops chewing, looks down at the table then back at me, and shakes her head. "I doubt that. That's just the way they are."

For a couple of minutes, we don't say anything and the house is so quiet I can hear the refrigerator humming and some katydids starting up their singing. Then Shelly looks at me and starts laughing and then I start laughing and we're having a good time laughing at each other, our bellies full.

"We sure showed them, didn't we?" she says.

I pop another pickle in my mouth and nod.

"It's gettin' dark in here," she says and she gets up and flips on the light in the kitchen. She goes to the hallway and flips on that light, then the one in the living room. She takes one of Aunt Carla's white lace doilies from the coffee table, sticks her tongue out at it, puts it on top of her head, and starts whirling around. I'm following her now, still laughing, making goofy faces at her.

Shelly kicks off her sneakers and glides on her bare feet from the living room down the hallway. She stops in front of Uncle Will and Aunt Carla's bedroom, opens the door, and goes in, flips on the light. When I catch up to her, I see she's standing there with her arms crossed in front of her. The white doily is still on top of her head, though it's slipped a little to the back of her scalp. She's staring at their bed.

"I bet they had sex before they went out," she says.

I look at the bed. The blue chenille bedspread is almost on the floor and the sheets are rumpled and the pillows look like two limp sandbags butting up against one another. It really looks like they just climbed out of bed and didn't look back. Anyway, when I hear that word—sex—I'm not sure what to think. I know just enough (which isn't a whole lot) to feel as confused as I do excited, especially when I try to get any picture in my mind of how Uncle Will and Aunt Carla could possibly be associated with such an act. I mean, just thinking of both of them naked (which I understand you have to be if you're going to do this) and climbing all over each other is enough to make me shudder.

"I can smell it," Shelly says, shaking her head.

"You can smell it?"

"Yep. I sure can."

I sniff the air. I can't smell anything. I wonder. What in heaven's name does it smell like?

She goes over to the chest of drawers and picks up a bottle with some amber-colored fluid in it, unscrews the silver cap, and sniffs. She makes a face like she's smelling sour milk. "Good God. This perfume she wears." And she holds it up in the air and squirts it. "It's awful!"

A little of it wafts my way. The air in the room is already stale and warm and now it smells sickly sweet. I put my hands over my nose and mouth. I don't want to be in here anymore. "Then quit spraying it all over the place!" I say. "Quit. C'mon, let's get out of here."

She twirls around, laughing, and puts the cologne back on the dresser. I'm already turning to leave when she comes behind me and puts a hand on my head, patting it lightly. "You're right. You're way too young for this stuff."

I don't like the way she says this. She makes it sound like I'm practically a baby. And this after I've managed to pull off what I would consider to be a pretty daring rescue from that rattler.

"Leave me alone," I say, bolting out of the room and down the hallway. She breaks into a run and comes after me.

"Remind me next time we come across a snake to just leave you standing there like the scaredy cat you are!" I yell at her. I've got my hands on the knob of a closet door where I'm planning to dash in and get away from her, but when I turn it and push, it doesn't open. At this point, I'm fed up with Uncle Will and Aunt Carla's proclivity for locking doors and then I see there's a thumb lock beneath the doorknob, so I turn it and push again and the door opens.

I stumble inside what turns out to be not a closet but a room almost as big as our bedroom. I hear Shelly's footsteps and the movement of the door's rusty hinge as she follows behind me.

The first thing I see, against the far wall, is a tall wooden gun case with glass doors, and inside are several hunting rifles belonging to Uncle Will. Over to the right, just beyond the open door, is a table, something like a desk I think, with several cardboard boxes on top and some old, yellow newspapers and dusty magazines. Beneath the table I see what looks like a small wooden bed. I think of Skeet, the old yellow lab they had who was run over last year by some high school kid driving a Pontiac too fast, and I think maybe that bed had once been his back when he was a pup.

"We're not supposed to be in here," Shelly whispers. "This room is off limits. They told us that."

"I thought it was a closet," I say. "Anyway, why are you whispering?"

"I don't know," she says out loud, shrugging. Then she starts laughing. "Cause we're not supposed to be in here, doofus."

Next to the gun case I see more cardboard boxes stacked on top of one another and I peek inside one. I see some old hats—a couple of ladies' hats, one with feathers and some sparkle, and a simple straw hat whose weaving has begun to come apart around the rim. Another box holds some old framed photographs, a little wooden music box, and a couple of books on poultry and cattle.

It seems every house has a room like this. One of those places where things nobody uses or wants anymore are put in boxes. And by the time we die and get put in our own box in the ground, we've left behind all these discarded bits and pieces of our lives. In boxes.

Alongside this stuff is a stainless steel clothing rack. Three suit bags hang from it, zipped up. On the floor behind the clothing rack is a row of boots: knee-high rubber boots, a couple of pairs of working boots with thick soles like Uncle Will wears when he's on the road, and an old pair of cowboy boots. The floor is dusty and a grimy, bare window, which sits just above the boxes, offers some fading orange streaks of what's left of daylight.

"Where's the light? I don't see a wall switch," says Shelly. I can hear her, but I can't see her.

I look up and see a bare bulb hanging from the ceiling fixture and a frayed string dangling beside it. I reach an arm up, my fingers grazing the string. I try again, this time jumping, and I'm able to grab the switch and pull. It's a dim light and I've startled a moth, which seems to have come out of nowhere and is now fluttering in circles around the light.

I go over to the gun case and touch its brass door handle. I expect it will be locked so I shouldn't bother to turn it, but I do. To my surprise, it opens (that's Uncle Will for you). He's got some real beauties—a couple of nice 12-gauge pigeon shotguns and a slim-looking beaut of a Daisy BB gun. I touch the wood handle of one of the pigeon rifles and let out a whistle.

"Shelly, come look at these," I say.

"Holy Moses," she says, but she's not standing where I can see her. I close the door of the gun case and turn around. She's on her knees beneath the table. Her hand is resting on the small wooden bed.

"You gotta see these, Weldon."

I come closer to where she is. She reaches in and pulls out something—I can't tell what it is at first—and then scurries out from beneath the table and stands up, holding it out in front of her. She holds it up high, and it's long and narrow and trails off in a stiff loop down around her feet. I recognize the tan-colored scales, the dark zigzag line running all the way down the length of its body. My spine tingles. It's just the skin. No head and no rattle.

"Whoa. Where'd you get that?" I say.

"Bunch of them down here," she says, pointing to the little bed.

I crouch under the table and look inside. I see them now. All kinds. Long strips like a drawer full of belts rolled and stacked—brown ones, gray ones, and those with that dark diamond mark.

I pick up one that's dark gray with white stripes. It's dry and smooth. The ends of the scales are stiff and rough. Beneath it I see another brown one and still other kinds below. I'm getting goosebumps on my arms looking at them. And I'm beginning to wonder more and more about Uncle Will. I mean, I always figured he was crazy enough, but this is a kind of crazy that makes me wish I could watch and see how he does it.

"We're living with a snake killer," I say.

Well, this is enough good news for my sister. She starts running in circles around the room, waving the snake skin in the air like it's some kind of banner in an Easter parade. "Wooooooeeee," she yells. "Don't make Uncle Will mad. He might skin you alive!"

Well, I don't happen to think she's that funny because as far as I'm concerned you never know about Uncle Will. Anyway, Shelly zips back around and squats down next to me. I'm looking at the little bed again. It's made of pine. The sides are high, running end to end in a straight line, but the ends are rounded with some nice curves and scallops carved on their tops. I can feel the trace of someone's hand trying to make a fine and fancy thing.

"Is that a baby's bed?" I say.

"Looks like it."

"But they don't have one."

Shelly nods. "They used to. I think. Aunt Carla was pregnant same time Mama was with you."

"Maybe it died," I say. We look at each other. Shelly laughs. Like she's nervous.

"Probably," she says. "Or maybe they just didn't want it. I don't remember Mama saying what happened." She ran her finger in circles on the wood floor. "Maybe that's why we get on their nerves."

It's a mystery to me, one I feel repeating itself over and over in this room.

"Anyway," says Shelly, leaning forward and touching the cradle, "let's take the snake skins and spread 'em all out on the floor."

We start quietly laying them out on the dusty floor side by side. By my count, there are eighteen of them and, lined up as they are, they look like a rug woven by a blind man, but an inspired one at that. There are dark zigzags against white stripes and dots and dark diamond shapes and colors of muddy brown and gray and tan. And some places, mostly around the edges, look like they've been touched by a sunset. When I hold a piece of skin in my hand and raise it up to the light, I can see my fingers through it.

When we're done, we sit and look at them for a long, silent moment.

"Wow," Shelly says at last.

"Yeah," I whisper back. "What do you think he's going to do with these?"

Shelly shrugs. "Beats me. Maybe he's saving up to make a pair of boots. You ever saw a pair of snakeskin boots?"

"No. Have you?"

She nodded. "Long time ago. I went shopping once with Mama, back before she got sick. We were looking for shoes and the store had this pair of ladies' snakeskin boots. And I thought they were the most beautiful things I'd ever seen. The shoe guy let me touch them." She smiled. "I'll never forget that."

"How many snake skins you think it takes to make a pair of boots?" I say.

"I don't know," she says. "A lot, I imagine."

We stare back down at them for another long, quiet moment.

"I wonder how he kills them," I say.

"Maybe he shoots them with one of those rifles of his," she says.

Well, I can tell Shelly doesn't know much about shooting. "Nah," I say, "there wouldn't be anything left of the snake if he shot it. It'd explode in a million pieces."

"You think he cuts off their heads?" she says. Her face looks a shade lighter, kind of sickly.

"Of course. They're not gonna just fall off by themselves."

"Oh God," Shelly says. She covers her face with her hands. Her body shudders. "We better put these away." She starts picking them up one by one. As I'm helping her, I see that she's getting real nervous. I guess the snake skins have spooked her.

After we put the skins back, she tells me to get the Elmer's Glue. I look at her like she's crazy, but she tells me to hush and do it. I know by the sound of her voice she means it and this is no time to pick a fight with her. As I race around to our room, it suddenly occurs to me all the nutty things I don't understand about Shelly—like how one minute she's as daring as a parachutist doing tricks on the wing of an airplane, but when something spooks her, she goes all out in the opposite direction and gets as nervous and agitated as someone dancing on hot coals.

While I race around to our room to get the glue, she's already switched off the light and I hear the door to that room slamming and the turning of the thumb lock. I go to the cigar box I keep by my bed. It holds my pencils, a few crayons, and the glue she wants. I can hear her running around and realize that she's going now from room to room turning off all the lights she'd turned on earlier.

She's in the kitchen when I hear her hollering. "Where's that glue, doofus? Hurry up!"

"What's this all about?" I say as I give her the glue. She hurries past me to the kitchen door and opens it and starts squeezing glue into the corner of the screen where she cut it. She dabs it with her finger and smoothes it, and then she latches the screen door and closes the kitchen door, but she doesn't lock it. Just like it was before we broke in. She starts clearing the kitchen table and rinsing our plates, but instead of putting them in the dish rack she dries them and puts them back up in the cabinet where they were before. She wipes the counter-tops and wraps the bread, shaking her head as she puts it back in the bin. She returns the butter and jam and pickles to the refrigerator. It's like watching a movie run backward. I finally ask her what in the world has gotten into her and she just tells me that we need to be out on the front porch pretending to be asleep when Uncle Will and Aunt Carla get home.

**

When I think about it now, it shouldn't have come as much of a surprise to me that, as daring as Shelly was, she would rather ensure arousing Uncle Will and Aunt Carla's guilt (and maybe, if possible, a little pity). The years had taught us a great deal in terms of balancing a daredevil streak with the cold, sobering rush of fear. The kind of fear that teaches you its usefulness but also carries the malignant spell of its weight. I don't know if looking at those snake skins is really what scared Shelly that day or if it was something else.

It almost worked, except for that damned doily. It fell off her head when I ran from Uncle Will and Aunt Carla's bed-room and she started after me and she forgot all about it. Then there's the obvious fact that we'd left behind a lot less bread and jam and butter and pickles than before. And, as if that weren't enough, in her haste, Shelly forgot to put her sneakers back on. But there we were, huddled like a couple of sleeping pups on the front porch when they pulled up in that Buick, the high beams cutting the chilly darkness. And I remember hoping that Shelly would be right; that they had drunk enough that they'd be kind to us, maybe even amused to find us there. Well, she was at least half right. Uncle Will was pretty mad, but Aunt Carla did shush him, saying it wasn't right for us to have been out there so long, sleeping sitting up with our backs against the door. As they ushered us inside, Aunt Carla whispering and laughing, Uncle Will grumbling that we were nothing but trouble, I was grateful our reprieve would last at least through the night.

**

Not long after she turned seventeen, Shelly packed up her suitcase one early Sunday morning, came over to my bed, and woke me to give me a hug and tell me she was leaving. She had already quit school before finishing her senior year and had been working in an ice cream parlor, sacking her nickels away until she could afford a bus ticket.

"Stay away from the hooch," she told me, "and find yourself someone nice to marry." She didn't say where she was going, but I later learned she ended up in Little Rock, twice-married and, by her latest account, trying to stay off the hooch herself. We keep up with the occasional phone call or Christmas card. It's just enough for me to notice the distance.

I wouldn't say we're unhappy exactly...

But this was all before I started thinking about what it meant to sin and to be sinned against and how it all seemed to fit so neatly in a house that never felt like home, where a man and a woman stumbled in the darkness as they undressed, dazed and emboldened by too much gin and dancing; where I tried that long-ago night not to hear all the ways a woman's laugh can also sound like crying and how a man can plead with a woman; a man capable of skinning not just one poisonous snake but a lot of them, as if doing so would end all doubts about what he could do right beneath the Good Lord's pale blue sky.

102

So Shelly got away, but I stayed. Maybe she was braver than me for leaving, or maybe I was brave enough to stay. I'm not sure, but it doesn't really matter anymore. I think maybe she'll come back someday. I know how things get under a person's skin and stay there and I believe the place she sees outside her window every day is not the same as the one she carries around inside her.

Anyway, I've got a nice pair of ladies' snakeskin boots I had custom-made from that boxful of snake skins I claimed for myself when Uncle Will and Aunt Carla passed away, so if Shelly ever does come back, maybe she's likely not to feel as sorry.

The house is mine too, now. Only these days, I call it home.

Patterns

It's January and the fuel truck didn't come today. Supposed to come tomorrow, Mom says. She's been putting off ordering it. I think it's because payday isn't until the end of the week. She hasn't been feeling well the past few days either, says it's some kind of stomach bug. Lately, trying to ask her about something has been like sticking your nose in a hornet's nest.

It's cold in the house and it smells like gas. We have gas stoves—big gray boxes that make heat from a row of grates. My brother, Billy, says the gas flames are what heat the grates. The flames make all kinds of colors—blue, orange, red, yellow—and when they really get going, the grates look like little towers with windows on fire. When the grates are cold, they're black in the places where the flames have touched them.

But I can't think about how cold I am right now. I have to do a sewing project for Home Economics—a class I don't really like much. I'm making a dress. I've never made a dress before. Mom promised if I get it cut and pinned she'll help me with the sewing machine. It's Monday. I've got to finish it by Thursday and even on her better days, I know my mother isn't very good when it comes to deadlines.

After our supper of canned spaghetti, I go upstairs to my bedroom and start unfolding the brown paper tissues of my

McCall's pattern when Billy appears at my door.

"Let's get out of here," he says, blowing into his hands and rubbing them together.

**

The vinyl bucket seats in Billy's Sunbird are freezing. White fluffs of cotton stuffing poke out along ripped seams. Just as he slips the key into the ignition, I hear a tiny animal sound. It feels too close and too far away at the same time. It makes goosebumps on the goosebumps I've already got.

I recognize that sound.

"Don't!" I shout. "It's the cat." The one that belongs to anyone in our neighborhood who fills a dish with milk and sets it on the doorstep, which is what I did five days ago. So, of course, he keeps returning. Billy's engine must have had some warmth on it from earlier.

His wrist pops away from the keys.

"Dammit, Shar."

He gets out of the car. By the time I get out, I see he's already slid beneath it, legs levered like a grasshopper's. I hear the cat's squealing mixed up with my brother's cursing. Something clangs against the car's metal guts. Then plop. Four dark paws on the concrete. The cat lets out a high-pitched moan that stretches into a yowl.

"Damn cat. Shoo! Get outta here!" Billy is mad.

I glance up at the cold black sky, stars like grains of ice gleaming, my breath making white clouds. The weatherman said something about icy rain.

The cat scurries out from beneath the car, leaps over my sneakers, and is quickly swallowed by the dark. A shiver runs up my neck and shoulder blades. I think—actually, I know— this is not a good sign.

**

At least it's warm here in the 7-Eleven. First thing, Billy heads for the *Playboy* magazines and I go to the comic books rack to get the latest on Veronica and Archie. Then we start loading up on chocolate milk, beef jerky, potato chips, Twinkies.

A few minutes later, we meet up at the cash register. The cashier is bagging our stuff. Billy asks for a pack of Winstons. The cashier—a burly guy with a naked girl tattooed on his hairy right forearm—hesitates, eyeing Billy.

"You old enough?"

It's Billy's face. He has the kind of face that looks like it got left behind while the rest of his body grew and got hairier.

"Of course," he says, pulling out his wallet and waving it at the man. Then he nods in the direction of the store's parking lot. "That's my Sunbird out there."

The cashier, still looking at Billy, hesitates a few more seconds, shrugs, then grabs a pack from the shelf behind him and slides it across the counter.

Billy lays out some dollar bills and starts fingering quarters and dimes, his oil-stained hands looking dirtier under that yellow-green light hanging above the register.

"How much?" he says, squinting at the total on the register.

"Six dollars and fifteen cents, including the cigarettes," the man says.

Billy turns to me. "You got any money?"

I dig in my front jean pocket, pull out a dollar bill, leftover change from my cafeteria lunch money. Billy quickly snatches it. He continues counting. The cashier's fingers drum the counter.

"Five dollars and forty-eight cents," Billy says. He looks at me. "You need to put something back."

"Why me?" I say, pointing to the cigarettes. "Why don't you put those back?"

The cashier's eyebrows start dancing up and down.

Billy grabs the Twinkies and marches back to the aisle where I got them.

The cashier glances up at the ceiling and back down, sighing.

I get a bad feeling again, like earlier.

As Billy is turning out of the store's parking lot, he reaches inside his coat, pulls the pack of Twinkies out, and tosses it to me.

"Keep your mouth shut," he says, gunning the engine.

**

Wes's truck is parked in front of the house.

"Looks like lover boy is back," whispers Billy.

"Oh yay," I say.

We get out of the car, me wondering where the cat is, me hoping the cat will return. My boomerang cat. Ten times better than Boomerang Wes.

Once inside, we keep our coats on. Billy bolts for the living room. Time for *The Red Skelton Show*. I hear voices in the kitchen, my mother laughing softly. I sneak a peek. Wes is canoodling her, his head close to hers, like he's trying to make her swallow it or something.

I guess Mom has heard us, because then she says: "Sweetie? Billy? Sharon?" She appears in the front hall, tucking back some strands of hair that have come loose from the straw-colored knot she made this morning.

"Hey, Mom," I say, my hand in my coat pocket, fingering the cellophane of the Twinkies. "How you feeling?"

She eyes me sideways. Her cheeks are pink. Mom's been married twice. The first time, she was seventeen and it didn't last very long. She once compared her divorce to getting off the train tracks just in time before the train mows you down. The second time, she was in her early twenties and that's how Billy and me came about, but we were both still crawling on all fours when our father left. I don't remember him, but Billy does. Mom now says—or I should say she swears, because she actually got out her Bible once and put her hand on it—that she will never get married again.

"Oh, I'm fine, fine, you know. Just fine," she says now. That's three *fines* in a row and then the corner of her mouth inches into something like a smile.

Then Wes appears behind her. He winks at me, lifts a palm, and stiffly teeters it sideways like a puppet waving. What a weirdo.

"Hey, Wes," I say, meekly returning his wave.

Why is he back?

I give Mom one of my *what's going on here* looks. Something I learned from her. I guess she gets it because she starts rubbing her hands together like someone waiting for bad news. Then she slips a hand inside her shirt and starts fingering her right bra strap back up her shoulder.

The three of us stand there like strangers at a bus stop. I wonder how long Wes will stay this time. I don't understand what my mom expects is going to be different. I mean, besides the same old conniving, canoodling Wes.

Oh, what a relief it is, from the Alka-Seltzer song, bounces out from the living room.

My mother points at the door, which I now realize is not closed all the way.

"Don't let the cold in," she says, hugging herself.

I give the door a good shove, making sure I hear the *click* that says it's closed as I watch my mother leaning into Wes and it feels like there's suddenly less of her standing there.

✳✳

I spread the first page of the pattern out on my bedroom floor. The paper is very thin, like a dried-up leaf. Side 1 of the dress is upside down as I look at it and it's on the left side. Side 2 is right side up, opposite Side 1. In the middle are what's called the front yoke and the back yoke. They look like floating islands. And two more pieces that are curved at the bottoms. These are pockets. Mrs. Filmore, our Home Economics teacher, says we're going to have a fashion show and everyone has to bring in their dresses and model them. When I heard this, I actually got sweat in my armpits. I cannot imagine doing this. I can just see Dorie Adams and Shirley Jenkins laughing and pointing. I hate them. I'm thinking of coming up with some kind of excuse, just in case. It's got to be something Mrs. Filmore will buy.

Well, here goes. I have scissors. I have my mother's sewing box; its cushioned lid has all these holes from straight pins. I have some yards of cotton printed with green and yellow flowers. Mom let me pick it out myself at the fabric store.

I unfold the cloth, spread it out on the floor, make it smooth with my palm, then I place Side 1 on top as I try to remember Mrs. Filmore's instructions about following the dotted lines of the pattern. I start pinning the paper to the cloth, which is actually harder than Mrs. Filmore makes it sound. With the first three pins I manage to stick myself and get little blood drops on the thin brown paper, then while trying to dab at the blood with my saliva, I manage to make a tear in the paper. So I blow on it, hoping it will dry. I'm still wearing my coat and I remember the Twinkies. I pull them out of my pocket and can see by the lamplight that the package got a little beat up and some of that creamy white filling is starting to ooze from one of the cakes.

I happily forget about pins and scissors and torn patterns as I rip open the package and take a bite of Twinkie. I like to get to the part where the creamy hole is and I can work the cream out with my tongue. It's so good.

I lick my fingers clean of cake crumbs and after what seems like a long time, I finally finish pinning Side 1, which has my sticky fingerprints all over it now and is puckered by the pins. I unroll and spread out another piece of the fabric and lay out the pattern for Side 2 next to Side 1, then I start pinning Side

2 to the fabric, slower this time so I don't stick myself, while humming and singing *Plop, plop, fizz, fizz, oh what a relief it is*. Finally, I'm ready to start cutting. I get the scissors but as I look at the pattern, which reminds me of a highway map showing several lanes of traffic, I can't figure out which line I should follow. Then I remember Mrs. Filmore saying to follow the solid one, not the perforated ones, and don't forget the "V" and "W" notches, so that's what I do, although a couple of times, the scissors slip while I'm trying to do the notches. But I keep cutting, thinking that it's a good thing we got more material than the pattern called for.

By the time I cut past the armholes and get to the shoulders, I start hearing not just my scissors cutting the cloth but a larger noise; an all-too-familiar noise.

Wes is yelling. My mother yells back.

Side 1, Side 2.

"Absolutely not! I told you I don't want to."

That's my mother's voice. Clearly, she's upset.

"Oh, baby, come on now, let's...let's just..." That's Wes. But his voice goes down a pitch and I can't hear the rest of what he's saying. I stop cutting, letting the scissors slip from my grip. There's a pause and then the voices start up again. There is a lot of high-pitched talking going on, but now I can't hear the exact words—though I suspect there's plenty of the foul, four-letter kind being used. I mean, Wes and my mom—well, they've never been very keen on what you might call polite conversation.

Now I hear Billy. He's adding his voice to the piled-up voices of Mom and Wes. He wants Wes to leave. Good luck with that. I know pretty much only one thing about Wes. Well, two actually. One: he's a creep. Two: if you tell him to zig he will zag. Just because.

Funny. I could probably understand what they were saying if they weren't yelling. That makes me think of the strangeness of sounds at a certain level, like my boomerang cat's meow. Or like when someone whispers, you can really hear them?

I mean, you can even hear words that aren't there?

**

I hear a faint crying noise and raise my head. How long have I been asleep? When I raise my face, I see my cheek has left a moist impression on Side 2. By the lamplight, I see my handiwork. My stomach hurts.

I hear it again. That cry that seems both far away and close. My boomerang cat?

It must be late. The house is quiet. And still cold. I get up from the floor, feeling a movement, a swirling from outside and when I look out my bedroom window I see—much to my surprise—that it's snowing.

"Wow," I whisper. The weatherman didn't mention snow. Maybe he was surprised too?

Then I hear that crying sound again.

I go to the window and put my hand against it. The glass is freezing, of course, and icy globs of snow stick to it, making a pretty pattern. In a halo of brightness from the streetlight, tiny dots of snow gather and swirl. I look down and see that Wes's truck is still here, the snow covering its hood and roof like powdered sugar.

But Billy's Sunbird is gone. I don't remember hearing him leave, but I guess he must have got pretty mad, yelling like he was earlier. I wish he would've told me he was leaving. I mean, he'll be back. This isn't the first time he's up and left like this. Especially when Wes shows up.

I still have my coat on, but now I button it up good and pull my limp gloves from the pockets and slip them on. I open my bedroom door. It's dark, except for a nightlight my mom likes to keep on in the space at the top of the stairs.

I slip out of my bedroom and down the stairs. I'm moving slow cause it's dark all over except for bits of light and shadow from the moon and the streetlights leaking in through the windows. Sometimes, it feels like we live in a house made of thin sticks that one good gust of wind could bring down.

I get to the kitchen, where I open the fridge. I hold the door open for the light as I reach into the cabinet for a saucer.

The snow is coming on real good now. Why couldn't we have had this at Christmas? When it snows, everything familiar feels different, like it's become something else. It always makes me feel like pretending.

I tip the milk carton into the saucer and watch it pool not quite to the edge. I touch my tongue to the cold milk, my eyes closed. I've heard cats can feel a lot through their whiskers—they're like little antennas and they can feel pain there too. Then I think about how cats can see in the dark, how their eyes glow, and so I pretend as if I'm feline enough to make my way through the darkness as I close the refrigerator door and start going from the kitchen, through the dining room, then the living room, and then...*bump*...the recliner. I freeze as a bit of the milk sloshes and spills onto the toe of my shoes. My genius brother has left the footrest open.

I finally make it to the front door and outside and as I put the saucer down on the front step here he comes, meowing as if he can smell the milk a mile away, and he brushes his body against my legs—back and forth in an excited pace, as if he were saying *thank you, thank you, I love you*. I stroke the top of his head, which is wet with snow, and whisper, "You're welcome."

I touch my gloved fingers to my cheeks. I can feel the snow falling on me now. If Billy were here, I'd go wake him up and tell him to come see this. Maybe wherever he is, he's watching it too.

Then, I hear a noise so loud I swear my heart stops and I pound a fist against my chest because I'm afraid I might stop breathing. I realize it's the loud, quick chirping sound of a siren and then I see a squad car drift by our house, its top lights whirling around, their beams cutting across the lawn, the sidewalk, the front of our house and the trees, like a wobbly moon going off its axis. The first thing I think of is Billy's in some kind of trouble. Bad trouble, and my stomach goes as tight as a fist. But then the police car passes our house and stops across the street and two houses over from ours. The place where the old couple lives. I don't know their names. The old man likes to hack away with a noisy edger at what's left of some shrubs in front and I've seen the woman in the backyard, hanging laundry or sitting in one of those foldout chairs, reading or sometimes sleeping. She's always wearing a big, gray sweater, even when it's warm. I've trick-or-treated their house. They like to give away Reese's Cups. That's about all I know about them.

Two policemen get out of the car and are walking to the door when, from behind, I hear our door opening and when I turn around, I see Wes. He's wrapped in my mother's blue chenille bathrobe. He's yawning, running his hands through his hair, which is going in several different directions at once. Boy, does he look like an idiot in that robe! I can see he has his jeans and a T-shirt on underneath it, and his shoes, without socks.

"Hey there, girl," he says. "What in the world you doing out here?"

"Hey," I say back, pointing down at the cat. "I heard him meowing."

He shakes his head and sees that I'm staring at him. I can't help it.

"What're you looking at?" he says, like it's perfectly natural for him to be walking around in a woman's bathrobe. He digs in the front pocket of his jeans, pulling out his lighter and a cigarette. He flicks his lighter close to his face until a flame pops, and then I see the orange glow of the cigarette and a puff of smoke vanish into the cold air.

I turn back around, looking across the street again. "Nothing," I mutter, not caring whether he hears me or not. I bunch my coat up around me.

An ambulance comes up the street now, its red lights turning, spilling red reflections across the white lawns and sidewalks.

"What's going on?" Wes says. He's standing beside me now. I see lights coming on in the house across the street and then a couple more houses light up.

"The old couple in that house," I say, pointing to it. "I guess one of them got sick."

I sit down on the front step, stroking the cat's head. The milk is nearly gone, but he's still licking the saucer, making it click against the concrete with that hungry tongue of his.

Wes sits down beside me, drawing his knees up to where he can rest his arms on them. The sleeves of the robe are big and drape across his pants' legs. He's got the collar of the robe turned up against the cold. Then he looks up at the sky, raising his hands and spreading his palms.

"Well, golly," he says. "How about this? Too bad it ain't Christmas, huh?"

I shrug and slowly nod. Mom once said something about Wes during one of those times when she was mad at him. I can't remember exactly what it was, but it was like he was just a kid in a grown-up person's body.

Across the street, the ambulance has pulled out a bed with wheels and a couple of guys are rolling it up to the door. Wes and I watch as he flicks ashes.

"That don't look good," he whispers. "Might be worse than sick."

I'm feeling a little dumbstruck, so I stay quiet. I remember seeing my grandmother in her coffin at the funeral. She looked like she'd been carved out of chalk.

Wes draws on his cigarette again, releasing another cloud of smoke and icy breath. He clears his throat. "Your mama's feeling a little better," he says, like he's answering a question I hadn't actually asked.

I don't look at him, but a few seconds later he nudges me gently with his elbow.

"You hear me?" he says.

I turn and look at him. "Yes."

We're both quiet for a minute, then he leans forward, tightening into a crouch, like he's trying to make himself smaller.

"What if I was to tell you..." he begins with a whisper, "it's, you know, just what they call morning sickness. What about that?"

I keep my eyes on the old couple's house, waiting, those words gathering like a storm in my brain. I shrug. I have nothing to say, but I suddenly feel like someone sitting in a room that's flooded, and the water level is rising.

Wes is chuckling. Then he nudges me with his elbow again. This time, I don't like it and I say stop it.

"Oh, whoa," he says, his voice fake with surprise. "C'mon now. You don't gotta be like that."

The door to the old couple's house opens and the police come out, followed by the ambulance guys who are wheeling the bed out with a body on it, covered in a sheet, followed by the old man, still in his pajamas, with what looks like his wife's big gray sweater thrown over his shoulders. He's gripping it tightly around him with both hands. His head is down, moving back and forth. I can't tell for sure, but it looks to me like his hands are shaking.

Wes goes on to tell me that it's his intention to propose marriage to my mother and then he says "*Voila*, instant family" as he slaps his hands together, laughing in that funny way people do when they're nervous. I almost feel sorry for him.

And then, I find myself wishing, hoping, *wishing, hoping* that Billy will pull up in his Sunbird, and the fuel truck will come tomorrow and the house will be warm again, and I close my eyes and imagine all the stoves fired up and glowing, my cheeks flushed and sweating, blood flowing to fingers and toes, and I'll take my pinned and cut Sides 1 and 2 to Mom who will be bright-eyed and vertical again, ready to start the sewing part and otherwise set things right *and* she also *absolutely, positively* will not be pregnant.

When I open my eyes again, I see the old man climbing into the back of the ambulance, his hands still hugging the empty sleeves of that sweater.

I look down and, out of the corner of my eye, I see the hem of my mother's robe brushing across the top of Wes's shoe, which he is nervously tapping up and down and up and down. I cannot see the future or anything like that. But I think about the dress and if I don't get it done, Mrs. Filmore is going to put a big fat "F" on my report card. I wish I knew what I was doing. I tried to cut the notches right, tried to keep to that solid line. But the paper is so thin, so full of confusing pathways, and I know I will never be able to be careful enough not to keep messing it up.

That's me, a fluke with a big capital "F" to go alongside the F which will no doubt appear on my report card. Suddenly, Wes chuckles, then he says softly "Hey, mama" and at the same time I feel cool hands on my eyes and realize it's Mom. She kisses the top of my head and murmurs "Hey, bug" to me. I whirl around like I'm falling and she will catch me. She puts her arms around me. I smell tobacco and feel a brush of wool—she's slipped Wes's shirt on over her gown. I bury my face against her, right there in the place just below her boobs, the place where she holds all her secrets.

Close to the Bone

It's my fiftieth birthday and I'm having lunch with my big brother, Grady, in a posh restaurant sixty stories up in the air with a view of Manhattan skyscrapers and drifting clouds. A day earlier, I descended from the clouds after flying first-class—compliments of my brother. I looked out my window, cloud-gazing almost the whole trip, my Coca-Cola wobbling now and then on my tray table whenever we *encountered turbulence* (what a phrase!) to use the pilot's words and, even then, I couldn't stop thinking about the bone.

I found it several days ago while taking my afternoon stroll in the wooded park near where I live. I was walking my usual path when the toe of my sneaker hit something hard and round and there, half-buried amid the carpet of brown and gold leaves, I saw a bone. I picked it up. It was large, mottled with gray, and mossed in parts.

Earlier that morning I had gone to see the Monster who, as I tell my brother, is doing remarkably fine these days. My visits with him are weirdly quiet and uneventful, and I had been thinking about that when my toe bumped against the bone. As I held it, turning it in my hands, I felt its muted, rough beauty and I thought of how time was reshaping it into something beyond death. The discovery folded itself into my day, creating an odd fusion with my visit that morning and my sense of the Monster as a weakening, wheelchair-bound mortal.

Monster is the name we use for our father. Since suffering a stroke several years ago, he now resides in an expensive nursing home, doesn't recognize me as his daughter, never asks about Grady, and has absolutely beguiled the nursing home staff with his charms. They think he's a puppy. Grady finds this interesting, even amusing (it's Grady who is paying for the nursing home), and—he says as he crumples his white napkin in his hand—*ironic*. I can see the whites of his knuckles when he says this. Looking at his hands always reminds me of that long-ago day when he lifted them out of the dishwater.

We finish our entrees of *sole meuniere* quietly. With my tongue I tease out a bit of fishbone attached to a delicate piece of buttery flesh and I think of how light and hollow fishbones are and the weighted feeling I had in that moment when I found the bone. I'm about to tell Grady about this and my flash of clarity about the Monster and life and death when our waiter shows up in his cheerful white shirt and green bowtie and carefully places in front of me an exquisite little cake with lavender icing. My name, Nellie, is written in a beautiful calligraphy of thin lines of chocolate. A single pink candle planted above the *i* shyly flickers.

I look up at Grady, who grins sheepishly at me before pointing at the candle, urging me to make a wish. I oblige him, only pretending to make a wish because I don't know what I would wish for. Candles and wishes have never been my thing. With a puff of my breath, the flame is gone. In that instant it occurs to me that Grady will not want to hear about the bone.

My brother is treating me to a lavish birthday lunch at this five-star restaurant in the clouds. It's one of his favorites. He knows the chef, a big fellow with a rust-colored beard and tattoos covering both arms. His deft fingers can arrange edible violets around a silken square of duck liver mousse sprinkled with peppercorns he's sliced himself with one of those precision-engineered Japanese chef's knives that even Amazon won't sell for less than $200.

My brother's the one with the money. He's a very sought-after investment analyst with a top New York firm. He does venture capital things too, he says. He once explained it all to me, but I have to confess I still do not understand. I think of him basically as a magician with other people's money from which he manages to bank plenty for himself. And it is money my brother understands; money which motivates and liberates him; money which allows him to be the gatekeeper to the Monster's fate when every month he clicks a button that sets in motion a transfer of funds that pays the nursing home to keep the Monster there.

As for me, well, two marriages—need I say failed? A fragile relationship with a grown daughter, twenty years of therapy, an office job that skidded into the ditch some years back so I quit. Now I work for myself at my potting wheel, my hands coated in wet clay as I shape and spin my vases and bowls and plates. In the winter, I knit hats and scarves and sell them along with my pottery. I just barely make rent and groceries most months but I like what I do and scraping by is not something unfamiliar to me.

I'd like to be in love again someday. This time, more peacefully.

I see the world despite our father's shadow and sometimes, I think, because of it. Because of him I crave both solitude and tenderness—things I cannot reconcile. Because of him, I look beyond the horizon line of any given view, always on the lookout for what isn't there.

✷✷

After lunch we go to Grady's apartment—also in the clouds—because he wants me to see it, although I'm not staying with him during my visit. Instead, as part of my birthday, he has gotten me a room at the Waldorf. For me to enjoy all by myself, he says. But I find the pricey comfort of my suite a bit nerve-racking. And this morning I had to go to the ATM machine to get cash which I then took to the concierge, asking him if he could break a twenty into ones and fives so I have tip money for all the bellhops and the maid and, of course, room service. Grady insisted I do room service. It's ridiculously expensive.

I think the real reason my brother put me up at the Waldorf is because he doesn't want me to stay with him. I don't take it personally. My brother—with his money and his pain—has built a perimeter around his life; it's invisible and impenetrable. I have no doubt it began during those days when we were at the less-than-tender mercies of our father—the days and years following our mother's unexpected death. We were all he had left, but he could find no comfort in that.

I mentioned Grady's hands and dishwater earlier. What happened was we were cleaning up the supper dishes one evening following a particularly nasty meltdown by the Monster that had involved several plates getting broken, lots of yelling about how worthless we were, then the screeching of tires as he drove off into the night, leaving us alone for three days. Grady was twelve. I was eight. We felt relieved that the Monster had gone. We were left to clean up the mess he made. Grady began washing what was left of the dishes that hadn't been broken. I was drying. I had to stand on a step stool. I remember that moment when he lifted a plate out of the dishwater and I saw his hands. They were bright scarlet and had huge welts all over them. The tips of his fingers were blistered, but when I looked at his face it was calm and quiet and it was like he was a thousand miles away. I was afraid if I said anything he would disappear. He later said it was the dish detergent. He was allergic.

**

After I found the bone, I took it home and cleaned it. I laid it in the sink, squirted a bit of dishwashing liquid on it, ran some warm water, and carefully washed it. The image of Grady's red and welted hands came to me—how quiet the house was after the Monster had stormed off into the night, how we carefully picked up pieces of broken plates and put them in the garbage and then later counted how many plates we had left.

That wasn't the first tirade for the Monster. We knew it wouldn't be the last and that he would return. But in the interim, it would be peaceful in the house and we could do whatever we felt like. I watched as Grady rubbed lotion on his hands—I offered to do it for him, but he wouldn't let me. I guessed it hurt for someone else to touch them. We rode the bus to Treasure City where I discovered how deft my brother's hands were at pocketing little things—paper dolls, yoyos, Bic ballpoints, packs of gum—and how clever he was about picking out one thing we'd pay for like some notebook paper for school, while everything else was stuffed in the inside pockets of his coat.

We knew it was wrong, but we never talked about it because that would have made it real. We found refuge and a quiet power in being elusive, undetected, emerging into the bracing chilly evening with our pocketed treasures. Over the years we learned ways of being subversive that served us well. We could look the Monster in the eye and lie to him if we thought it would keep the peace and keep us safe. We were careful about laughing at things that might draw attention to us because that usually meant trouble too. Still, sometimes Grady couldn't hold it in. He'd mutter something he shouldn't have and the Monster would hear it (he had hearing like a dog's) and...well, let me just say that Grady was the one who took our father's blows and somehow kept going. I never saw him raise a fist at the Monster. He once told me that the Monster hadn't always been a monster. That something had happened. Our mother's death? He thought maybe, but he didn't know. He has memories I don't have; memories of walking with him along a creek with only the sound of water flowing and how he liked picking out rocks that he could pitch into the water, making them skip one, two, three times across the water's surface. Like a grasshopper. He loved doing that, Grady said. Grady remembers watching him prepare to throw the rock, turning his body just so, making this almost magical flip of the wrist that would send the rock out onto the water like a dancer.

As I washed the bone, I kept wondering what animal it had once been a part of. A deer? A fox? Someone's dog? It was almost six inches across. I ran my finger from the ball-shaped socket across to the left where it dipped into a deeply recessed cavity. I placed my thumb there and it fit perfectly. I held it up before me, soapy and dripping. It had to be a joint bone of some kind—hip? Shoulder? I wondered what had happened. The bone looked like it had been torn away—violently severed is what I imagined. On its underside I could see a constellation of tiny porous holes. Where was the rest of it? I tried to imagine a fight between two animals there in the park not far from a pathway I faithfully walk every afternoon, but the severing of bone and limb felt like too much. I placed the bone on a towel and gently patted it dry and as I did, I felt a shiver—the kind people say happens when someone walks over your grave.

**

My brother's apartment is sleek and modern with pale wood floors, a white sofa, two white leather chairs, a white kitchen that hardly looks used, and not much else. No pictures or knickknacks, no clutter of any kind. The moment I enter in my frumpy clothes and tangled brown-gray mane, I feel like a blotch on a white sheet. He likes the dining room best, he says, because of the window running from floor to ceiling and right to left—a glass wall, really—offering a vertiginous view of the glimmering, dusky buildings of lower Manhattan from fifty stories in the air.

"Something, isn't it?" he says.

"Wow," I whisper. Standing in front of the window, I feel unsteady; if I lean another inch closer, I'll be falling into all those buildings. I step back, smiling, because this smarts a bit, all this austerity, this glass and steel aerie with its quietly programmed thermal harmonies. I feel as if the floor could vanish beneath me. This is what my brother calls home.

"Sit," Grady says. "Want some water? A glass of wine?"

"Water," I say as I retreat to the sofa, sinking down into it. My feet barely touch the floor. I check the cuffs of my sweater, making sure I don't have any stains that could leave their trace.

Years ago my therapist told me that, when I get too much noise in my brain, to picture myself reaching for a volume button and turning it down. I close my eyes and try to conjure this image as my brother sets a glass of chilled water on the marble coffee table.

"Nellie? You okay?" he says.

I open my eyes and smile. "Yes, of course. A little tired is all."

I lean forward and take my glass of water, gulping it down as Grady settles into one of the white leather chairs across from me. We sit there in silence. Now the volume feels too low, I think.

"How's Claire? You ever see her?" I ask. Claire is Grady's ex. He met her when he first moved to New York and after two weeks of dating, they got married. Nine months later, it was over. Marriage, Grady had declared—flatly but emphatically—wasn't for him.

I could tell by his face he didn't like the question.

"No, not lately," he finally says, shrugging. "I think she has a new boyfriend."

"Oh," I say.

Grady nervously drums his fingers on the arm of the chair.

"I found a bone," I suddenly say.

My brother looks at me, eyes wide. "What?" he says.

"A bone," I repeat. "I found a bone. In the park. Took it home, washed it."

He looks at me, nods. "Really?"

"Really."

"What kind of bone?" he says. It's perfunctory, his response. Almost as if he fears I might start spinning one of my weird tales from my "close-to-the-earth life," as he once called it.

"I don't know. I think it's a joint bone. From an animal."

Grady chuckles, a little uncomfortably. "Kind of weird, isn't it?"

"What?"

"Keeping a bone like that. Why would you want to do that?"

Once my brother and I shared a language of unspoken gestures, nods and signals that helped get us through those days with the Monster. But after Grady started high school, things changed. We fell out of the rhythms of our days we knew as siblings when we used to gather things like acorns, abandoned birds' nests, the vacant, papery husk of a hornet's nest. We were intrepid explorers who occasionally pilfered things. Grady used to love watching a spider patiently working a line of silk into a web. We could get lost in the world that contained us, gave us space to breathe and forget. But inevitably, I think now, we became like two branches of a tree growing in opposite directions. By the time Grady got to high school he couldn't be bothered with nests and spiderwebs anymore. Or me. This stung. I loved Grady. I thought he was brave. But as we grew, we had to learn how to be with other people, which meant pretending you were as normal as you thought they were.

I smile at him now. "I don't know. It's like a piece of sculpture. You know me." I shrug, I laugh.

He nods, smiling a bit warily, crossing his arms.

"You creative types," he says. "Too weird for me."

I'm making a vase for him for his birthday, which is four months away. I hope to surprise him. Looking around, I think the place could use a little something.

"So," he says again, "how you doing money-wise? You need any?"

I certainly wouldn't mind having less of a cash-flow problem.

I smile, count to ten. "No. Thanks."

**

As I said, I live near a park—the one where I found the bone. I rent a little house—a cottage, really—and it's just me. After several years of living alone, I'm thinking of getting another pet. I used to have a black lab, but he's gone now. I still remember cradling his face as he lay dying, feeling his last breaths in my palm. So old and littered with tumors. Basil, I called him. After the herb. Maybe this time I'll get a cat. Or perhaps a dog and a cat. Get them as babies, have them grow up together. I've always liked the idea of doing that. They would know one another not as *cat* and *dog* but as that other creature whose skin and fur smells they recognize, their bodily presence—one to the other—ever familiar, braided and cocooned as limbic memories. They will know one another's heartbeats.

A few miles in the opposite direction of the park is a river and sometimes in early autumn when it's especially pretty, I drive there and sit along its rocky banks. I just like the peace of sitting there. Leaning into the sounds of wind and water, I sense the presence of animals trying to hide; strange sounds emerge—rustlings from a nearby copse of trees, a scuttling or shuffling that precedes a hush.

There was a bramble-like hedge in front of our house where Grady and I took refuge once, waiting out one of those episodes when the Monster was shaking the rafters. There were some birds in the hedge—Grady pointed to the hairy ball of a nest embedded in the hedge's thin branches and there was lots of nervous back-and-forth chirping and tweeting. Then the birds grew suddenly quiet, and it took me a few seconds before I realized why. Through the crosshatched density of the hedge I could see the shadowy figure of a cat who lived in our neighborhood—one of those vagrant types that subsist door to door, milk bowl to milk bowl. Anyway, there we were—me, Grady, *and* the birds, all of us quiet and still, all waiting for the threat to recede and my heart was a bird's heart, quickening in the brush.

⁎⁎

The Monster cradles the bone in his hand, turning it over, hefting it in his palm.

"You say this was in the park you live near?" he says.

"Yes."

"I didn't know you lived near a park."

"I told you before." I say this easily and quietly.

"I forget," he says. He gently taps his head with a balled fist. "My noggin, it's a little off these days, you know." He looks down at the bone. "Poor thing," he says, almost whispering. He shakes his head.

I nod slowly. Where is the *Monster* we once knew? The one who crept into the dreamscapes of our nights, whose disturbed presence could be felt in all the places he was absent? The one who ignited silences? What had happened to all that violent sorrow?

I think of how Grady laughed nervously at the thought of the bone, then felt the need to change the subject. But the Monster calmly regards it and, like me, he wonders what kind of animal it's from and what might have happened to it.

As I got ready to leave Grady's place, he asked me why I still go to see the Monster. He couldn't understand why I'd want to do that—sit with him, visit with him.

His question surprised me, although I guess it shouldn't have. I said he seemed different now—that the spark we knew and feared had dimmed to meekness. It was like sharing time with a nice stranger. But the truth is I'm not sure myself why I go to see him. It's something beyond forgiveness for me. I don't know. It's like a quiet freedom I feel, being with him now.

Grady just looked at me, puzzled. He cautioned me to be careful. When I hugged him goodbye and thanked him, he held me very lightly. Grady's not much of a hugger.

My father hands me back the bone and I slip it into my little canvas tote bag. I stand and gather my coat from the back of the chair and as I slip one arm in a sleeve I see him grip the arms of his wheelchair and heave his body to standing. He blinks, his old eyes flickering and simmering like a blind man feeling along a wall as he walks.

"Turn around," he says, softly. I do so and he takes my coat, holding it as I carefully slip my other arm into the waiting sleeve. I can hear his breathing, rough and unpleasant. He gently pulls the coat up and around my shoulders, patting and smoothing them with his palms. I stay very still. Then I feel his hands go away, hear a rustling and shifting as he lowers himself back into his wheelchair.

"You coming back soon?" he says.

As I said, it was Grady who took the Monster's blows. I have known only the absence of his touch—a liminal space of vigilance and distance.

"*Be careful,*" Grady had said.

I turn and look at the Monster, his face—the patch of gray whiskers covering his sagging jowls, those eyes of his knit with wrinkles and puffed from either too much sleep or not enough. He looks at me, waiting, his hands folded in his lap.

I zip my coat, take my handbag and the canvas tote with the bone—oh, the weight of that bone.

"Next week?" I say. Why did I say that? I've been coming once or twice a month, picking a time when I felt like it.

He nods, smiling weakly. "Thanks," he says. "Okay."

＊＊

It isn't until I get outside the nursing home that I realize I've been holding my breath. There's a bench at the left of the entrance and I decide to sit for a moment. I can still feel his hands on my shoulders.

The sky is a chilled gray streaked with orange, thin wisps of clouds gathering. It's late afternoon. I need to stop at Aldi and get a few groceries. I cup one hand inside the other. My fingers are cold so I dig for my gloves in the pocket of my coat and slip them on, and as I do I start laughing. It comes out of me like a hiccup.

Next week? Really?

Maybe I'll drive to the river first before it gets dark. I'll sit for a while, listen for the sounds I like—the furtive movements of animals, the water sluicing rocks.

I start to stand but my body feels too heavy for my legs, so I sit back down. I wait for the moment to pass—for the spell to unwind and dissolve. The late afternoon light feels so strange—amber fading into cold.

I wait. My heart a bird's heart.

Some Kind of Day

The lump on Louis's temple was coloring to blue and purple and it hurt. But he didn't care. It had been worth it just to go after that chicken. If only they could have stayed to see the fire trucks. He pressed his nose against the back window of the bus as it pulled away, watching the same chicken he'd come within seconds of nabbing flapping its wings atop the spinning red light of a police squad car.

Louis, his mother, and his sister, Elena, were on their way to his grandparents' house for their once-a-month Saturday lunch. A ritual his mother never hesitated to declare as something she did more for them than for herself.

They had started their trip with the No. 12 bus from Pelham Parkway all the way across Bronx Park and the Grand Concourse to University Avenue. Nearly an hour, and boring too, thought Louis, until they passed the zoo where he could see its arched green entry gates carved with animals. At University Avenue they switched to the No. 3, which dropped them off a few blocks from his grandparents' post-war red brick apartment building on Undercliff Avenue.

It was a sweltering June day. The Watergate hearings were all over the airwaves, on TV and in the newspapers. Nixon was on the ropes. That's how Louis's mother described it, fuming about what a liar he was as she listened to the hearings on the radio.

When they finally arrived, the first thing everyone noticed was Louis's lump. But he couldn't wait to tell them everything; how they were waiting for the No. 3 when around the corner from Fordham Road came a truck carrying chickens. The rear tire blew out, making a sound like gunfire. The truck tipped sideways, sending crates of chickens sliding and toppling all across University Avenue. Several crates broke open and chickens went running in all directions. Excited, Louis went after one and as he was chasing it, he ran smack into the elbow of an old man struggling with a small canvas trolley filled with groceries. Canned goods, dinner rolls, bananas spilled forth, along with the old man's curses as Louis, head throbbing, struggled to get to his feet. But not before he felt his mother's hand grabbing his shirt collar.

"Ah, so that's what those sirens were about," said his grandfather. "The chicken trucks coming from the farms upstate."

"There were fire trucks and police cars everywhere," exulted Louis.

He winced as his grandmother grazed the lump with a gnarled index finger.

"Oh dear," she said. "Next thing you know it'll be a bloody nose."

"Not to worry, Rose," said his mother. "He's already managed that."

Then his grandfather inspected it. "Mmm...quite a bruise. This your first one?"

Louis shook his head. "Not really. But it's been a while," he said proudly.

"Smells good, Grandma," said Elena. "Lasagna?"

Rose clasped her hands, nodding. The smell filled the small apartment, made too warm by the oven. The table was set. There would be other food too. Louis figured probably pot roast or corned beef.

When they sat down to eat, he couldn't wait to continue his story about the truck. But no sooner were they picking up their forks than his mother started in again about Nixon and those tapes.

"So what?" said his grandfather. "He's right on this one."

"What?" said his mother. Normally, Louis would have taken this as his cue to keep quiet. But he jumped ahead, describing the spectacle of chickens, how there must have been hundreds of them.

"There were not," said Elena. "You're exaggerating. Maybe twenty. Or twenty-five. Thirty at most." She licked her fork.

Louis thrust his chin in her direction, watching his mother out of the corner of his eye.

"You didn't have time to count them."

"Hush, Louis," said his mother. "I can't believe this," she continued, turning to his grandfather. "If Maury were here, he would be shocked to hear you."

Louis saw his grandfather wince, his face briefly flickering into pain.

Louis was only two when his father died. When Louis started third grade, his grandfather thought he was old enough to be told the simple truth, so he took him aside one day, but as he started to explain, he choked. All he could say was heart attack. He wasn't able to say how Louis's father was riding a taxi across the Brooklyn Bridge on a chilled autumn afternoon, and before the cab had made it across the river into Brooklyn, he had collapsed. The cabbie told police he hadn't noticed anything until he pulled up in front of the address Louis's father had given him. It was the apartment of a girlfriend from his college days.

"You never heard of executive privilege?" his grandfather said, trying to control his voice.

"Grandpa, one chicken was chasing a woman carrying a bag of apples," Louis broke in. "And another one was pecking at the police car's lights."

"Privilege?! Hah!" said his mother, lifting a forkful of lasagna to her mouth.

"Really, Louis?" said his grandmother. "Now that would be a sight."

Louis nodded eagerly. "It was, Grandma."

She was wearing thick bifocals that made her eyes look like big nervous fish eyes. Rose was losing her eyesight. Her doctor gave her a couple more years, but there was no stopping it.

"Oh Rose, please," said Louis's mother. "Don't encourage him."

"The boy's got a rich imagination," his grandfather said.

"He's actually correct this time, Grandpa," said Elena, much to Louis's surprise.

"Well, that's very *judicious* of you, Elena," his grandfather said. He insisted on engaging his grandkids with the use of a well-cultivated vocabulary. Elena crooked her head a little, grinning as she eyed Louis.

"What's that mean?" Louis said to his grandfather, who responded by raising a finger, nodding.

"It means to be fair-minded," he said while shooting an icy glance toward Louis's mother.

His grandmother rose from her chair, went to the kitchen, and returned with a large platter of what Louis now saw was roast chicken. Glistening, carved-up pieces of breasts, wings, drumsticks, and thighs that previously would have made his mouth water.

"Anyway, you've gotten in enough trouble today with that *imagination* of yours," said his mother, glaring at him as she impaled a chicken thigh with her fork. "Do you realize," she went on, pausing for emphasis as the table hushed around her, "I would have had to take you for all kinds of shots if you'd gotten your hands on that chicken? Especially if it'd pecked you with its filthy beak." Here she lifted her knife and pointed it at him, shaking it up and down. "And I mean *shots*, young man. Not just one. A whole lot worse than that lump you've got now."

Louis looked down at his plate. His fifth-grade friend, Mario Lanzotti, once got bit by a dog and had to have five shots in his belly. Still, he'd never heard of anyone getting bit by a chicken, much less dying from it.

He ran his fork over the square of lasagna oozing cheese beside a clump of limp string beans. If chickens are so dirty, he thought, why were they eating them? But, as his grandmother speared a drumstick and set it on his plate, he figured it wasn't exactly the right moment to point this out. He still couldn't get over how the chickens had brought everything to a halt, squawking and strutting like the whole street was their chicken yard. Now, looking at the drumstick on his plate, he felt depressed.

"Enough," said his grandmother.

"Fine," said his mother. The word landed like a thud. She had put down her knife and fork and was gnawing a thigh bone.

His mother was always too hard and, at the same time, falling apart about something. She would go on and on about how she was only trying to keep him and Elena from harm, which, as she was fond of reminding them, was a nerve-racking job.

He traded glances with Aunt Loretta, who winked at him. She had greeted Louis earlier, inspecting his bruise with her usual air of dreamy distraction, marveling at its colors, smiling as she dangled before him the little beribboned gold box from Fazio's with a half-dozen cannoli. Three, she said—holding up the requisite number of fingers—with chocolate chips. His favorite.

Aunt Loretta was his father's sister. She wasn't married and worked as a court stenographer. She maintained a degree of arms-length politeness at these lunches and usually didn't have a lot to say. Her dark hair was piled on top of her head and she spoke softly, like someone half-awake.

She had the same dark eyes as Louis's father. And like Louis too.

He chewed his food. The lasagna was good. He figured the chicken was too, though after today he didn't feel like touching his. Everyone ate quietly now, in between bits of conversation where his mother and grandfather warily circled one another regarding the finer points of Nixon's treachery. He watched his grandfather lift his fork to his lips, his hand wobbling, his eyes like a basset hound's—watery, wrinkled—his gray hair like coiled wires. His grandmother carved her food as she vacantly stared elsewhere. He felt sorry about her bad eyes. His mother helped herself to seconds of everything. Elena said she would be taking clarinet lessons come summer and when her grandfather asked about her grades, she reminded him about making the honor roll at the end of the school year, though she was careful not to make it sound like bragging. She would be a high school freshman in the fall.

"What about you, Louis?" said his grandfather.

There wasn't much to brag about. He'd managed to pass fifth grade. It probably wasn't worth mentioning how he'd ended the school year with two trips to the principal's office, first for getting a black eye from Marvin Gramisch and the second time for giving a bloody nose to Neil Kranowsky. There might have been a third trip if he had been caught pocketing the $5 bill he'd seen fall from the back pocket of Stuart Logan's jeans one day in geography class. So far, so good. He still had the $5 tucked in his sock drawer.

"Two trips to the principal's office," said his mother.

"We dissected some frogs," he said. "It grossed all the girls out." He pictured frogs everywhere, rising up in the biology lab, hopping off the tables and down the backs of all the girls' dresses.

After lunch, everyone moved to the living room. The grandparents retreated to their recliners and Louis sat between them on a worn tweed ottoman. His grandmother nervously tumbled her fingers in her lap. Elena sat on the green brocade sofa at a cautious distance from their mother. Now and then, Louis would look at her with his eyes crossed. She'd roll her eyes at him, trying to keep from laughing. At last, Aunt Loretta passed around the cannoli on little paper plates with a paper cocktail napkin tucked beneath. When she got to Louis, she held out the plate for him to take and winked at him. "You get one with chocolate chips," she said, "on account of that bump." She lightly tapped his forehead with a fingernail. Louis smiled and thanked her. Then, she kissed each one of them on the cheek and left, saying in her hushed voice that she had plans for the evening.

"I just bet," Louis's mother remarked when Aunt Loretta closed the door behind her. Elena once told him their mother had her suspicions about Aunt Loretta because she wasn't married. When he'd asked her why, she had responded that it had to do with being jealous. An answer that was about as clear as mud to Louis.

Well, as far as he was concerned, the day had been a success, beginning with the chickens and—even with the lump and the mugging he got from his mother—resulting in this moment when he raised the cannoli to his mouth and teased out a single chocolate chip with his tongue. A few seconds later, it was gone. He could feel his mother's eyes watching him. "You're like a vacuum cleaner, Louis. For God's sake, slow it down." He remembered her gnawing on that chicken bone like it was her last meal.

The corners of Elena's mouth turned slightly upward. She lifted her cannoli and waved it at him until their mother turned toward her, at which point she slowly brought the pastry to her lips and sheepishly nibbled at it.

He stood to take his empty plate to the kitchen trash can, and, remembering his manners, offered to take his grandparents' plates too. They smiled, passing them to him. He greedily eyed an uneaten sliver of cannoli on his grandfather's plate. His grandmother squeezed his wrist, whispering, "You're a good boy." The balls of her eyes darted like quivering blips of

Morse code. The thick lenses of her glasses made red creases in the area between the sagging skin of her eyes and her plump cheeks.

He stole a glance at his mother. She was still eating her cannoli or he might have offered to take her plate. He didn't dare look at her as he walked to the kitchen where he dropped the plates in the trash, but not before lifting that leftover bite of pastry from his grandfather's plate and swallowing it whole.

He washed his hands at the kitchen sink, taking his time. They were talking about the Watergate committee and the senator with those fleshy jowls "like curtains blowing apart by a gust of air," as his grandfather described him.

He shut off the faucet, dried his hands against the back of his pants. He didn't feel like hearing more arguments about politics. He didn't understand how something so boring could get people so worked up. He looked over at his grandmother's chair and saw it was empty. She probably got bored too. Maybe he'd go look out the window from his grandparents' bedroom and watch the boats on the river. One of the things he liked best about coming here. He started walking slowly around the periphery of the living room when he heard his mother's voice.

"Where do you think you're going?"

He stopped, his shoulder grazing the wall. "Um, I was just going to look for Grandma."

"I thought she said she was going to the bathroom," his grandfather said.

Louis kept moving slowly along until he reached the doorway of his grandparents' bedroom. The door was half-open and he poked his head inside. No one. He slipped inside where the wood floor of the living room gave way to the carpeted dimness of the bedroom. There were two windows on the far side, their vinyl shades partly raised to let in the afternoon light. It was a dappled light, broken by the shadows of leaves from the tall trees outside. Louis went to the windows. In the distance, through the trees, he could see the Harlem River. He glimpsed a rowboat with two tiny figures in it, one of them working the oars. But no sailboats today.

This building where his grandparents lived had been built on a hill with a cement foundation that ran deep into the ground. So, though their apartment was on the first floor, the view was much higher from their bedroom window.

He spread his arms and swayed back and forth in front of the windows, dipping and weaving as if flying. He stopped, closed his eyes, undulating his arms, imagining himself gliding over the river. He loved these blinkered moments of freedom, how he always found them in the scarce half-light of his grandparents' bedroom, looking through those windows, through veils of leafy tree branches to the river in the distance, the sun's glaring light dancing off its surface. Here, his body, loose and willowy, seemed to ease itself into mysteries, sensations, experiences he felt just beyond his reach.

Now his gaze traveled from the river to the ground high above. Something caught his eye. A lumpish shadow. It was moving, as if rocking from side to side. He pressed his nose against the windowpane and followed the dark shape until he could see what looked like the familiar floral pattern of his grandmother's dress, her thick tan shoes.

He stepped back from the window. When he came out of the bedroom, he saw that his mother was thumbing a magazine. Elena's head was back on the couch, her eyes half-closed. His grandfather held his newspaper aloft, scanning its headlines.

"I'm going outside," said Louis. His grandfather turned and looked at him with an absent smile.

"Remember what I told you," warned his mother.

"I think Grandma's outside," he said. He didn't say he had seen her. At the back of the building facing the river. Where he wasn't allowed to go.

"Oh," his grandfather said. "I don't remember hearing her leave. But she likes sitting on the bench out front."

"Did you hear me, Louis?" said his mother.

He nodded.

"You're already in enough trouble."

With his back to her, he rolled his eyes as he went out of the apartment. He walked the linoleum corridor to the glass doors and went outside.

The bench beneath the building's portico was empty. He looked up and down the sidewalk. No one. He crossed the lawn along the side of the building until he reached the back. There, he saw the few yards of flat ground that ended at the border of a chain link fence with a sign that shouted *NO ONE ALLOWED BEYOND THIS POINT! THIS MEANS YOU!* On the other side, the ground extended another few yards before vanishing into a steep, perilous stretch of embankment jutted with rocks and pebbles and ruddy pieces of broken earth that ran several hundred yards all the way down to the Harlem River. After their father died, he and Elena had been forbidden by their mother to ever go back here by themselves. And now, here he stood, close to that perimeter, separated only by that chain link fence which sagged and buckled in places. He saw his grandmother, her floral dress hugging her plump frame, her body stiff as one of those mannequins he'd seen in a Macy's window. The sight of her was spooky, and Louis froze.

"Grandma?"

His throat felt like he had no room to make more of his voice. She didn't respond. "Grandma?" He forced his voice louder. "It's me, Louis."

She raised her head, her hands fluttering in front of her before she drew them in, cradling her elbows in her palms.

"Louis? Oh, Louis. I'm so glad you're here. Can you come and help me, please?"

This was a new kind of fear. Like touching something sharp in the dark. He cupped his hands around his mouth.

"Are you okay, Grandma?"

"Yes, yes," she said, weariness in her voice. "Just come, please.

Please, just come here."

His legs felt shaky. Slowly he put one foot in front of the other. As he got closer to her, he could see through the fence the flat ground receding into that steep slope. He felt a surge of energy. His breathing quickened.

His grandmother had one arm extended. Louis could see that her hand was shaking.

"Take my hand, Louis, please."

Her hand felt cold and wrinkled and soft and it was trembling. He took his other hand and ran it along the top of hers.

"It's okay, Grandma." He spread the fingers of his hand beneath hers and laced them through her fingers. She tightened her grip.

"I just walked back here," she said. "I've been back here a million times, you know, but I just couldn't tell where I was this time and I hit my foot on a rock and almost fell and..."

They walked as she kept talking, her voice a nervous warble. Louis glanced over his shoulder at the sloping earth, the deep curtain of trees, the river in the distance.

"...I couldn't see very well..."

They crossed the lawn and he led them to the bench, where he guided her to sit. She expelled a few more breaths of relief, then laughed again. She took off her glasses and rubbed her eyes. Little beads of sweat dotted her forehead.

"Thank you, Louis. That's what I get for just sneaking away like I did."

"You're welcome," he said.

"Did you sneak out too?" she said.

"Kind of," he said. "I came looking for you. I told them I was."

"You get bored? I wouldn't wonder, listening to all that arguing."

"I think they just like to argue." He thought if Nixon was in school, he'd be going to the principal's office a lot.

"I'm so tired of it all," she said. "The other day they canceled my favorite music program on the radio because of those stupid hearings."

They watched some cars go by, and a young couple strolling with a dog, holding hands.

"Will I get in trouble for going in the back? I'm already grounded."

She patted his knee. "Don't worry. As far as I'm concerned, we both need a cover story. So let's just say we've been here on the bench talking."

"Okay."

He thought about the trees and the river, how high it all felt, how dangerously close it felt too. Elena once told him how their father would hold her in his arms when she was small and point out the boats floating on the water, the clouds, nets of swallows circling in the air. Someday, when he was big enough, he would go back there and see for himself what it was like to just stand there for as long as he wanted and look out over things; how the earth dropped and spread itself out to the edge of the river. He thought about tomorrow, how he'd have to pass the day by himself in his room.

"Nixon," his grandmother muttered. "What a bore."

"Louis! Where are you?"

It was his mother, and when he heard her voice scrape the air, he jumped up from the bench.

"Be right back, Grandma," he said.

With a swiftness he could manage only when trouble was imminent, he sped around to the back of the building and right up to the chain link fence, his heart racing. With his palm, he slapped the sign with those shouting letters and then turned and ran back, imagining a thousand marauders thundering after him. He slid back onto the bench next to his grandmother and leaned his head back, his face to the sky, squinting his eyes against the sun as his mother, his grandfather, and Elena approached.

He sat up straight and looked down at his feet. They were almost completely flat against the sidewalk. He seesawed them—heel, toe, heel, toe.

"You didn't go back there, did you?" his mother said, her eyes squarely on him.

Louis bunched his mouth, still tapping his feet.

"Don't be ridiculous," his grandmother said, waving a hand as if batting an annoying fly away. "He's been right here," she continued, patting Louis's knee. "Right here with me, all along."

My Icarus

I had made scrambled eggs for her, but she just stared at them, wrinkling her nose. Her stomach had been bothering her for days; she'd been eating nothing but crackers and drinking 7 Up. A cluster of plastic grapes webbed with dust sat near the knob of her elbow. The table was crowded with stacks of dishes, goblets, mugs and cups and saucers.

I was getting anxious. It was almost ten-thirty. My cousin Tony was hoping to get on the road by noon. But Aunt Vera was still wrapped in her green chenille robe and she was digging in, nibbling a saltine with a vacant gaze. I could sense it. She was going *daft* on me.

But I was tired. And my nerves were already frayed. The night before, I had an argument with my soon-to-be ex, Hugh; this time about the checking accounts. It kept running loops in my brain.

I was more than ready for Tony to take over, but he had called and pleaded with me to help him get his mother on track.

"You know how it is," he said. "She likes you. Because you don't belong to her like I do."

Sixty years in this one house. A mid-century ranch in Rockville where termites feasted from within its walls, squirrels made nests in the attic, bagworms wove gossamer sacs in the backyard trees. The lawn was glorious with dandelions.

Ned, the estate handler I had hired to help empty the house, was busy at the other end of the dining table tagging Tupperware containers from thirty years ago, dishes, forks and knives and pots and pans my aunt and uncle had used since the 1950s.

"Like doing inventory for Ozzie and Harriet," he said.

I smiled as I continued sorting through a pile of books on the sofa. My fingers grazed a familiar green cover, sun-faded and starting to separate from its binding. I picked it up, recognizing it—Aunt Vera's cookbook, which she'd owned since before I was born (Copyright, 1941). I flipped through its pages, marveling at black and white images of roast beef, something called egg frizzle, a tomato-cheese soufflé, chocolate layer cake. A grocery receipt from 1992 floated to the carpet. Among the dog-eared pages were index cards with recipes handwritten in pencil, a museum postcard showing a painted landscape. On the back of it was Aunt Vera's recipe for eggnog.

I thought of the sticky notes all over my computer at work, and of the lists I keep, my user passwords, the folded pages torn from a daily calendar—all drifting like snowflakes from the pockets of my sweaters.

How many years before it would be me?

I want to keep all my marbles. I want them all there, knocking against one another, even as I'm dying. My mother's words, her wish for lucidity at death's door. She almost got it, except for those last days when her hospital room filled with the ghosts of family members I never knew and she kept mistaking me for the nurse. It's going on two years since she died and I think of our last words to one another as tangled threads neither of us could keep hold of.

Now, my fifteen-year marriage was effectively over, but— in the legal sense—stalled in the muddy zone of "separated, divorce pending." A sixty-five-hours-a-week job, two growing daughters. They're all legs and long hair. Their eyes glaze indifferently whenever I'm talking. Marty's fourteen, Gretchen her junior by three years. They maintain a softly-curdled resentment toward one another. But if one of them is away, the other always wants to know where she is and when she'll return. They cry easily. Especially since Hugh and I separated. Marty is struggling—or is it toying?—with whether she wants to live with her father or me. Of course, I want her to stay with me. Of course, I can't make her.

"Do you want this?" I said, waving the cookbook at Aunt Vera.

"That's my cookbook. I've had that since before you were born."

"Yes," I said. "I know. Do you want still want it?"

"Why don't you take it? I don't cook anymore."

Well, I wasn't much of a cook either. I set the book on the coffee table.

"I don't want to go anywhere," she said, fingering another saltine from the waxy paper cylinder. She looked around the dining room table.

"Why are all my dishes here?"

Uncle Leon poked his head from the kitchen.

"It's time to get dressed, Vera."

He and Tony were packing an ice chest for the long road trip to Wisconsin. Tony was a wreck. As a divorced (no kids) middle-aged professor of environmental science, he knew his days of long-distance caregiving by phone were over, but he wasn't looking forward to any of this. Last month, Uncle Leon nearly totaled the Subaru. It had been up to me to pry the car keys from his gnarled hands.

"You need to come now," I had told Tony in my best no-nonsense voice when I'd phoned him about the accident. "I'm running on empty."

I was the one who had listed and finalized the sale of the house; it was also me who had hired Ned to organize an estate sale. Finally, Tony called to say he'd found an assisted living apartment for them in Madison.

Aunt Vera rose, her expression furrowed with confusion. "What's the rush?" She had slender fingers with a slight palsy. Nails painted pale rose, knuckles freckled with brown spots, rivers of blue veins. The sash of her robe had come undone, showing her thin, sea-foam green nightgown. Her hair was a mess. Gray-blonde, the texture of cotton candy, and tumbling from its pinned-up state. I went and gathered her robe around her, picking up the ends of her sash and tying it.

"Time to shower and get dressed," I whispered.

She looked at me with her light blue eyes. She'd been a real beauty in her day. Blonde hair, blue eyes, a movie star's skin. She drove a red sports car to her job as a secretary at the State Department during the war—a war widow, it came to pass. The story was that Uncle Leon's pursuit of her had been feverish.

"Why are we leaving?" she asked. "It's too cold for a picnic. Anyway, I've got lunch plans." It was a cool and gray March day. The sky was thick with clouds. It still resembled a winter sky. But Uncle Leon's daffodils he'd planted back when I was in college had already popped. He was ninety now, Aunt Vera a couple years younger.

"You do not have lunch plans. Don't start making excuses," Uncle Leon announced from the kitchen. "We are leaving in less than an hour."

The muscles in Aunt Vera's jaw started twitching. "Tell him to leave me alone."

"Let's go," I said. I took her elbow, guiding her around a box of books and toward the bathroom. I felt my phone vibrate from my sweater pocket. Probably one of the girls, just waking up.

Aunt Vera slipped out of her robe and gown, tossing them on the closed lid of the toilet. Her backside was pale as the flesh of apples. She lifted a leg and gingerly stepped into the tub. She gripped my arm. She was shivering.

"It's so cold," she said.

I ran the water and let it warm before switching to the showerhead. She gasped as the water gushed forth, washing over her. I slid the shower curtain across. Warm steam filled the air. I pulled my phone from my pocket and saw there was a text. Charlie? For heaven's sake, why? Why now? *How about getting together for a drink? Maybe this evening? Just as friends?* He closed his message with a peevish smiley face.

Charlie was something of a good-looking man-child who, in the heat of one weird moment a couple of months back, appeared attractive to me. By then, Hugh had moved out and the emptiness I felt in the wake of his leaving had started eating a hole in my stomach. That day, Charlie was cleaning the coffee maker in the break room, and, I don't know...he just looked so sane and sweet, humming softly as he sponged the carafe, and the next thing I knew, I'd asked him if he'd like to go for a drink after work. I knew he was married. Down the rabbit hole we went. I happily lost my mind. Until one late afternoon, three weeks into it, I found myself driving to Olney for another tryst (he loved that word; I didn't). I was on a one-lane road. The sun was cutting through the trees at such a slant that it was burning my face and I pulled the car over because suddenly, I couldn't breathe. *I can't do this anymore*, I texted. *Sorry. Going back home.* But Charlie has a rather odd way of persisting—a meekness furred with cunning.

Forget it. I slipped the phone back into the pocket of my sweater.

Aunt Vera peeked from the shower curtain, waving a soapy washcloth. "Would you mind to wash my back?"

"Of course not," I said. She turned to face the tiled wall. I started washing her shoulders when there was a loud, insistent knock on the door.

"How much longer?" It was Uncle Leon. He banged on the door again.

Aunt Vera swiveled her head. "What in the world is going on?"

"It's Uncle Leon," I sighed. I dried my hands on my sweater and opened the door a couple of inches. He stood, hands on hips, in his cargo jacket and a baseball cap. His cheeks were flaky and red, scarred from where they'd sliced away melanoma.

"If you leave it up to her, we'll never get out of here."

I nodded. "We won't be long," I said, biting my lip.

"I'm not going anywhere!" Aunt Vera yelled. "I'm having a shower, and then I'm meeting Doris for lunch." Doris, who used to live next door, has been dead for five years. I smiled tightly at Uncle Leon as I closed the door. He hissed and stomped away. *Just get her out of the shower*. I had to get groceries, pick up my Lipitor at the pharmacy, take Marty shopping for something that she can't live without. What was it? I can't remember. A headache was starting at the base of my neck.

Aunt Vera was humming. I hated to do it, but I drew back the shower curtain, reached in, and shut off the water.

She blinked and softly gasped, her hands drawn up in tiny fists at her clavicle, her face dripping. "Well," she huffed, "could you at least pass me a towel, please? Before I freeze to death?"

I passed her the towel. She lifted one leg up and out, then the other, trembling as she clutched my forearm. She roughly toweled herself dry. I held her robe open as she slipped her arms inside the sleeves.

"I'm not going anywhere," she repeated as she knotted the sash of her robe. "I'm having lunch with Doris, then I'm going to read my *People* magazine on the patio and have a Pimm's. Everyone else can do as they please."

I stood, arms crossed, looking at her. A fading trail of morning light from the little bathroom window caught her face, the damp blue of her eyes.

"Aunt Vera, you know Doris isn't your neighbor anymore, right?"

Her fingers danced on the collar of her robe.

"So? Who cares?"

I cleared my throat. "I mean, you know she's, well, you know she's dead, right?"

She shot me a look—anxious, glaring, defiant. Then, just as quickly, her face melted.

"Jackie, would you have lunch with me?"

**

"What are you wearing today?" I said. No answer. She was sitting at her dressing table, holding her hands out in front of her, blankly staring at them.

"Aunt Vera?"

She looked up.

"What are you wearing?"

She frowned. "I don't know. Pick something out, will you?"

On the bed was a modest stack of clothes still on hangers that she'd chosen to take with her. Her suitcase, on the floor, had only a few things in it. I picked up the first outfit from the pile, a pair of navy blue pants and a yellow cable-knit sweater.

"How about this?" I said, waving it at her.

She was peering now through the partly-slit Venetian blinds of the window. She sat so quietly I thought something might be wrong. I put a hand on her shoulder. She looked up at me, her mouth twitching.

"Let's put these on, okay? Then I'll help you finish packing."

She nodded. I took the pants and held them close to the floor for her to step into. She pulled the sweater over her head as I slipped some white cotton socks onto her feet. We plucked bobby pins from the tangled density of her hair as I got a brush and tried to smooth it out and re-pin it as best I could.

"I was a widow when I married Leon, you know."

"Mmm..." I said, nodding. "I remember the story."

"My parents were worried. They didn't think it was a good

idea to marry Leon because he's Catholic. We were Methodists."

I gathered some strands of white hair from around her ears and at the nape of her neck, brushing them slowly.

"But it was during the war and, well, you *had* to be married..."

"Well," I said, "*vive la difference*, right? Look how long it's lasted."

She stiffened and grunted. "Maybe too long."

I was trying to make a French twist with her hair, coiling its stiff white strands around my fingers and tucking it in the back.

"You're still married, aren't you?" she said.

I stopped and looked at her face in the mirror, where her eyes found mine. She knew we were separated. Though it'd been ages since Hugh had seen her or Uncle Leon. She had taken my hand in hers the day I told her, saying it would be okay and I had loved her for being so cleanly reassuring.

"Well, I...we're..." I stuttered. "You remember, I told you. We—Hugh and I have separated."

The blue of her eyes seemed to float and shine as she took in my words.

"Oh," she said softly. "Yes. Of course. That's too bad, isn't it? I do remember your wedding. By the ocean?"

"Yes," I said. "Ocean City, as a matter of fact."

We were married just as summer's heat was fading. A blustery wind had nearly taken down a white tent we'd planted close to the shore.

I tucked a few more bobby pins in place and then she straightened her spine, leaning into the mirror, fingering her temples.

"Good god," she said, glowering at herself. "It's the bride of Frankenstein."

I smiled, patting her shoulders. She looked down, trailing a finger slowly over the wrinkled skin of her knuckles as if she were looking for something in its folds and I suddenly remembered Hugh daubing my nose with cake frosting on the tip of his finger, then hungrily kissing it away as the roof of our tent bubbled up and buckled in the wind.

"William was lost at sea, you know."

"What?"

"My first husband," she said. "His plane was shot down as he was flying over the ocean."

"Vera!" Uncle Leon shouted from the living room. "We've got the car packed. Vera?" He tapped on the bedroom door. "Let's roll. Now."

Her face dropped into a frown. "Phooey," she hissed. She picked up a tube of lipstick. Its brassy coating, tarnished and flaking, looked like something she'd owned a hundred years. She twisted its bottom and a tiny scarlet dome twirled up, less than a quarter inch of lipstick left. She made a couple of wobbly dabs at her mouth, then took a tissue between her lips, blotting then tossing it aside and, after touching a hand to the back of her hair, she stood, hand on her hip, and looked at me, suddenly smiling brightly.

"So, my dear Jackie. Where are you taking me for lunch?"

I started laughing, shaking my head. I couldn't help it. We were caught in a loop.

"What's so funny?" she said.

I put my arms around her. "Aunt Vera, I'm so sorry. I know this is hard." I patted the cushion of the stool. "Here, sit." I took her suitcase from the floor, put it on the bed, and started folding and packing the clothes she'd set aside earlier.

"How about shoes? Any other shoes you want to take?"

She just stood there, blinking, bewildered, the skin around her lively blue eyes sagging.

"I don't know how, Jackie," she said, settling back down onto the stool like a deflated balloon. "I don't know how to leave here."

**

"Give her a few minutes," I said.

I stood outside the bedroom, the door closed behind me, trying to calm Uncle Leon. He looked miserable.

"The traffic on 270. It gets pretty bad if you wait too long."

"Traffic is bad everywhere, Uncle Leon. This is Washington."

I slipped my arm through his, steering through the box-strewn living room, the dining room, the kitchen. Tony was outside, leaning into the back of the wagon, shifting and rearranging packed items for the trip.

"She won't speak to me," Uncle Leon continued, "and when she says anything, she won't look at me. And, lately, she eats like a mouse."

"It's a big move," I said, patting his arm. "Come on. Let's sit out front for a few minutes."

We stepped outside. On the right, just beneath the mailbox, there was a wooden bench. We sat. A small boy flew by on a skateboard and Uncle Leon sat up, alert to the noise. Little green strobe lights winked from the heels of the boy's sneakers.

"Who's that?" Uncle Leon said.

"A boy riding his skateboard."

"From which house?"

I squeezed his hand. "I'm afraid I don't know."

There was a time when he knew everyone on this street—who was sick, who was broke, who did what for a living, whose child had gone off to whichever war, who drank too much, and, of course, who was cheating on his or her spouse. But most of those people were gone now. And trying to figure out who was who in the neighborhood no longer endeared him. There was, after all, a thin line between curiosity and just plain nosiness and, well, Uncle Leon wasn't very subtle when it came to appreciating the distinction.

Tony popped his head out from the back of the wagon.

"All set," he said, raising two thumbs. He pulled the wagon door down, thrust his hands in his pockets, and trailed up the sidewalk toward us.

"How's it going with Mom?" he said.

Uncle Leon sighed. "We're waiting."

"Well, at least she's dressed," I said. "We've still got to finish getting her suitcase packed."

"You're kidding," Tony said.

"She's packed a few things," I said.

"She said she was packed," Tony said.

"I don't know what's wrong with her," said Uncle Leon. "We've been talking about this for months." He coughed and reached in his back pocket for a handkerchief, holding it to his face as he coughed again, then sneezed, then blew his nose. "She's been pretty agreeable. New apartment," he said. He looked up at Tony. "She was happy about being near you. Getting new furniture. Even a whole new wardrobe if she wanted."

He was right. She had told me last summer how tired she was of the house, the countless times in the past few years she'd dreamed of moving.

"Stubborn woman," sputtered Uncle Leon.

"Okay, I'll go talk to her," said Tony.

I touched his arm. "Give her a moment or two. I think she'll come around."

I walked with Uncle Leon to the side of the house where his daffodils were.

"I've hardly noticed these damned flowers for years," he grunted. "Can't hardly see them anymore anyway. Just a smear of yellow."

"They're the best thing about this place," I said.

"Pick some," he said. "Take some home."

I knelt and plucked a few. They were newly open, still cool and upright. I could put them in what is now *my* bedroom, where I sleep alone—maybe they'll soothe my insomnia of late, when I'm awakened by the absence of Hugh's breathing between my shoulder blades, or the larger vacancies that darkness can hold at two-thirty in the morning.

We circled back to where Tony was standing in the carport inspecting a huge snowblower—one of Uncle Leon's splurges a couple of winters ago after a blizzard dumped a foot of snow. He'd burrowed down the whole length of the street with it like a tunneling mole, loving every moment until neighbors complained—some with teeth politely gritted—about how the snow he'd pushed aside obstructed access to the sidewalks and paths leading to their doorways.

Tony was hoping to get a decent price for it. Ned had already tagged it. As Tony stooped, toggling and fingering various switches, knobs, and levers on the thing, Uncle Leon and I returned to the bench when Ned stuck his head out the front door.

"Uh…" He was smiling nervously, his eyes traveling from me to Uncle Leon to Tony before settling again on Uncle Leon. "I think you might want to come check on your wife."

**

Her cheek lay against the glass tabletop, her arms splayed across the table. At her elbow was the cookbook I had waved at her earlier. Ned told us she was inspecting a decaying birdhouse. Then she sat at the table, thumbing through the cookbook. A few minutes later, when he looked again, her head was down.

Tony was calling an ambulance. Uncle Leon got her to sit up. He cupped her chin with two fingers. "Vera, darling, talk to me," he said, with a voice he hadn't used all morning: tender, patient, clearly worried.

I brought a glass of water. She looked at it with a ghostly smile. She appeared confused, but not in a way that was distressful.

The ambulance arrived and the EMs examined her. Her heart sounded okay. Her blood pressure, though a little on the high side, was steady. She stared vacantly as they delicately probed her ears and shined a penlight into her eyes. Possibly a minor stroke, or perhaps some kind of aphasia, they concluded, recommending she be taken to the hospital. Her blue eyes had an odd glaze to them. Uncle Leon's shaky hand cupped her face as he vainly continued trying to get her to speak.

The EMs rolled a cot inside. We watched as a tense negotiation ensued. But it soon became clear she wasn't getting on the bed. They got a wheelchair instead. Uncle Leon got her to stand while one of the EMs wheeled the chair behind her. Then Uncle Leon put his hands on her shoulders, hoping to coax her into its seat. She wouldn't sit.

"Vera, please," he hoarsely pleaded.

Aunt Vera looked at him, but not like he was there. It was as if an opaque curtain hung between them. Suddenly, as one of the EMs was locking the wheels on the wheelchair, she raised her arms. The EM's eyes grew wide. He glanced at his colleague, who was half-smiling, half-frowning. He waved a hand in front of her. Nothing. She froze with her arms spread, her hands partly cupped, her thin fingers fanned, extended in delicate suspension, trembling. She waited.

"Mom?" Tony finally said, his voice barely above a whisper.

Uncle Leon stood before her, motionless. I had the impression he was through pleading with her.

"Dad?" Tony said.

One of the EMs looked at Tony, then me. He shrugged, I shrugged. Tony took a step forward, but froze as Uncle Leon entwined his fingers with Aunt Vera's, whispering her name. She put her other hand at his waist and started gliding sideways, tugging on Uncle Leon as if he were a heavy curtain. They swayed back and forth, puppets dangling on frayed strings. Their movements were stiff, halting, sometimes flickering gracefully as they danced—if dancing is what you could call it. There wasn't even so much as birdsong to accompany them. I could only assume whatever refrain they moved to had begun somewhere behind Aunt Vera's stony blue stare.

As Uncle Leon gained his footing, he took the lead, gliding with her in a muted struggle to move their dance from the patio to the living room. In the hopes, perhaps, of getting her out the door and into the ambulance? I shuddered at the thought of how they'd get through the patio door, navigating the bumpy glide path of the sliding screen without tripping. They didn't. Uncle Leon placed his cheek against hers and was whispering something and then they were waltzing, turning in fitful half-circles, weaving between packed boxes, the soles of Uncle Leon's taupe Mephistos erupting snaps of static electricity from the carpet. Aunt Vera kept her eyes closed. Her face glowed. She was a candle burning down to its essence.

As for poor Uncle Leon, he was maneuvering to keep the waltz going in the direction of the front door. I glanced over at Tony, who was now regarding the EMs—they were still out on the patio—with an imploring look. They merely shuffled their feet, eyebrows rising and falling, tight grins.

When I looked back to the living room, I saw that Aunt Vera and Uncle Leon were sliding away, their arms and legs awkwardly listing. They disappeared into the bedroom. Tony trailed after them. Ned came up beside me from the kitchen where he'd been watching. "She okay?" he said.

"Well," I said. "She can still waltz, apparently."

A moment later, Tony returned as the EMs stepped from the patio into the living room, dragging the wheelchair between them.

"Well," he said, shaking his head, "I guess she's okay. I'm sorry, guys. I don't know what to do."

"We can't force her to go," one of the EMs said. "Think she'll sign a waiver?"

"I'll do it," Tony said. "I've got power of attorney."

The EM passed the paper to him. "I'd still recommend her

doctor have a look at her."

Tony nodded as he signed. Uncle Leon appeared from the bedroom and everyone turned to look at him.

He swiped at his ear with a shaky hand. He appeared to be a little out of breath as he pulled a crumpled kerchief from his back pocket, mopping his face with it.

"She tells me she's hungry," he said. "Says she's starving. I guess we'll take her to lunch."

**

They finally got on their way late afternoon. Tony later told me that she seemed to get her appetite back when they took her to lunch. I said my goodbyes, hugging Uncle Leon first. He wrapped his arms around me—an embrace, a holding-on I hadn't expected. Then I put my arms around Aunt Vera, squeezing her small frame. She was like a warm blanket redolent with the fading scent of Guerlain. She gazed at me, the skin around her eyes wrinkling into a frown, a smile like a whisper, as she pressed her fingers into the fold of my elbow.

"Where are you going?" she softly said, breathing against me.

I had wanted them to go. I needed them to go. So many exhausting refrains had woven together these last months with them—*I'll take care of it, don't worry; I'll do that, okay? Have you got your grocery list? Take your pills; Give that to me; don't worry, I'll take care of you.*

And then they were gone.

**

It was the first week of June and I was having one of those days filled with the awful sense that time was marching on, but I wasn't prepared to move along with it. The divorce had become final. The day before, Marty came home from school

159

with a nose ring and a tattoo on her shoulder. We quarreled and then she announced she wanted to spend the summer with her father, who was now renting a condo (with a new lover, it seemed) in Virginia Beach.

Oh, Marty, let's not play this game, I wanted to say—or rather plead. But I know...go she will. I don't know. I just wish the things that hurt the most didn't always feel so inevitable.

Later that evening, I was making a cup of tea, waiting for it to steep when I spotted the cookbook on the kitchen shelf above the microwave. I had taken it with me when I left that day. I pulled it down, riffling through its pages. *Water Lily Salad. Cucumber Pear Aspic.* What a faraway world. I flipped a few more pages and started pulling out handwritten recipes on index cards. I wanted to save them. As I continued sifting through the pages, I pulled forth what I thought was another recipe card. But when I picked it up, I saw that it was the museum postcard I'd glimpsed earlier that morning. I looked at it. In the foreground, a plowman wearing a bright red shirt was busy tilling soil. Over his right shoulder, a blue-green seascape, where a large ship with billowing sails approached the shore. On the back of the postcard was Aunt Vera's eggnog recipe scribbled in pencil. Definitely a keeper, I thought. As I continued searching for more recipe cards, I came across a yellowed newspaper item, folded like a bookmark and tucked among a section of casserole recipes. I carefully unfolded it and saw that it was from 1943. It described how Lieutenant William Brendan, a fighter pilot, had gone missing in the South Pacific Ocean in November of that same year. It bore his photograph—a handsome man in his cloth overseas cap, dark eyes, a thin mustache, an easy smile. Oh, Aunt Vera, was this what you were looking for?

I was about to file the recipe cards in a little box when I looked again at the postcard. There, in small letters in the left corner beneath Aunt Vera's eggnog recipe, was the title of the painting: *Landscape with the Fall of Icarus.* By Pieter

Brueghel. Icarus. I recalled the myth from my college days—something about a boy with wax wings who flew too close to the sun. I turned the card back over and looked again at the plowman, slicing the earth with his horse and plow; below him, a sheepherder with his flock; trees and sky and that blue-green sea. Then I saw what I'd missed before—in front of that ship, Icarus's tiny pale leg sticking up in the air as he splashes into the sea.

There was a war, I told myself. Pilots falling into the ocean, or a thick forest of trees, or an open field where cows might graze.

Where are you going? she'd said to me. A question that stung all the way home. She encircled me with shadows, apprehensions, expectations; with spaces that must be filled. I still have too much to do, only now the days feel longer. And life itself feels so awfully brief.

I stuck the postcard on the door of my fridge with a magnet clip, promising myself to make a batch of that eggnog when the holidays rolled around. Now and then, the plowman catches my eye when I'm busy in the kitchen. He keeps his head down, keeps working, the blue-green water glazed by sunlight as the boy falls, disappearing with an inaudible splash into the sea.

The Things
She Said

Conner Pratt's life had returned to what it had been before he'd married Libby—a quasi-blissful mess, built around solitary habits of compulsiveness and days of yawning apathy. Only now, it had stretched and flattened since Libby died.

Libby's voice. Husky and edged with lazy laughter. These days, it danced in Conner's head. The sound of her Virginian horse country drawl, buoyant and teasing, still filled the inner chambers of his ear.

I've spilled a lot of milk, baby. A room full of cats couldn't lick it all up.

Stroking new whiskers, he waited, his car idling at National Airport, just outside Baggage Claim Area 6, for his daughter, Bethany, and her husband, Ryan, to arrive. The occasion was wedding bells for Bethany's best friend from high school, Trina. She'd asked Bethany to be her matron of honor.

The Brandenburg Concertos timbered pleasantly from the radio. The radiance of the late morning hour felt like something Conner wanted to reach out and touch. Instead, he stifled a yawn. He taught high school physics, and summer always made him lazy and anxious. He cradled his phone in case Bethany

163

texted. Their flight still showed to be on time. He looked up at the sliding glass exit doors, the bouncing reflections of sky and clouds drifting across the panes. Finally, through a hazy reflection of white clouds, he saw his daughter—that familiar mane of dark hair in a loose braid, a red T-shirt and denim shorts that ended at the knees, the pale flesh of her sturdy legs. She was dragging a big canvas duffel behind her, and she was clearly alone. She stopped, turned, flung the bag around in front of her, kicking it through the doors as they slid apart.

He got out of the car, waving and whistling to get her attention, smiling, feeling a surprising lightness at the sight of her.

She turned her head until she saw him, her face at once flickering from a kind of flat, muted sulk to happy recognition. She eagerly bounded toward him.

"Hi, Daddy. I made it."

She threw her arms around him. He kissed her cheek.

"Ouch. What's with the shadow?"

He rubbed his cheek. "Thought I might try out a beard," he said.

She shook her head. "It doesn't work."

He grinned sheepishly. "I'll put you in the 'no' column."

"Sorry. It makes you look swarthy and unreliable. You're not the type."

He grabbed the strap on the end of her bag and struggled to lift it onto the open hatch in the back of his Toyota wagon.

"Turn it," she said. She came around beside him and started shoving the bag until it yielded. He looked at her. She held up a hand.

"I know what you're thinking."

"Yeah? This bag really is bigger than you are. Jeez."

They got into the car and as he was cutting his wheels to pull away from the curb, he looked at her fidgeting with the seatbelt, struggling to get the buckle into its slot. He leaned over and pulled on it from up near her shoulder to slacken it.

"Try it now," he said.

She shoved the buckle again until it finally clicked in place, then pulled on the strap and glared straight ahead at the dashboard.

"Thanks," she mumbled as he pulled away from the terminal.

"So, no Ryan?" he said. She didn't answer.

"Bethany?"

"Okay," she finally said. "Ryan. Yes. Well, we had a fight. He decided not to come. A totally last-minute disaster. And I really don't want to talk about it. So, do you mind, Dad? The idea for the hotel is out. So, could I, you know, stay with you?"

"Can I ask how big a fight?" he said.

"Big enough. And then he had to..." She paused. "Forget it. Anyway, I want to unload the bag. Then I have to get my shoes for the wedding."

She sat up straight, taking a deep breath in through her lips, almost as if she were trying to whistle, and nervously started kneading her palms into her kneecaps.

"Sorry, Dad. I should have told you."

"So," he ventured, speaking softly, "how long were you..."

She sighed. "Oh, I don't know. I don't know. I don't care if I ever see him again. I never realized what a prick he is."

"Well, gee, Beth, I'm really sorry to hear that," he said. Ryan, the boy genius who liked bragging about how he got suspended in tenth grade for rigging the school's PA system so that the announcements were accompanied by the sounds of toilets flushing.

"So, that's that," she said, looking down at the tops of her sandals, her toenails with flaking turquoise nail polish.

Someone once told Conner the bigger the wedding, the shorter the marriage. Well, as far as he was concerned, Bethany's had been enough of a blowout. A bride of nineteen who'd wanted it all, of course. Over a hundred guests, a dress whose price tag could sustain a small village in Africa, not to mention the catering bill, the booze tab, the rental of the mansion with rooms that wound around one another like a carnival maze. And there was Libby as mother of the bride. The first time he had seen her after six months of separation. He had watched her from afar, in a moment of *déjà vu* as the rim of her champagne glass touched that of a man's wearing a summer jacket. The almost inaudible clink of those glasses a grenade going off inside his head.

Bethany slumped in her seat, her head leaning against the window, her eyes half-open.

"You're welcome to stay. If you don't mind a sleeper sofa," he said.

"You have a sleeper sofa? Since when?"

"Since moving. I wanted some different stuff. You might say I kinda downgraded."

"Mmm," she said. "What about...?"

"Later," he said.

"Okay. Sleeper sofa's cool," she said.

"So," he said, after a few less-than-breezy minutes. "How goes the barista wars these days?"

She bunched her mouth, sliding her eyes sideways. "I quit." She held up her hands. "Too many steam burns from the milk frother. And lousy pay, *and* the manager turned out to be a creep." She sighed. "I'm looking for something else."

Bethany's voice, her manner, her gestures, echoed those of her mother. Natural traits she could do nothing about. But for Conner, it was poignant and unsettling. *She's ours, Conner. I know she hates me, but she's ours. Please don't forget that.*

The drive was a half-hour via the GW Parkway to I-495, Friday traffic thickening and thinning as Conner's palms grew moist on the steering wheel. Bethany occupied herself by pulling out her phone, texting, calling friends, giggling; the sound of her laugh like a swimmer who'd gotten too much water in her lungs. And then she shifted to grim and quiet, muttering, "No. He didn't come."

At last, Conner turned onto his tree-lined street. It was a small thing, passing beneath one shade tree after another, but it gave him pleasure. He turned into the driveway.

"We're here," he said. It was a modest red brick house with two front windows bearing the ghostly outline of shutters and three concrete steps leading to a front door with fading yellow paint that had begun to peel. The door was on his to-do list of things to remedy. The house was one of a handful remaining in a neighborhood rapidly morphing into new two- and three-story colonials, stacked and square post-moderns, villas with balconies and terraced pathways.

"Cute," she said. "It's really small. Like that little guesthouse we had. Remember? In back of the big house?"

He nodded. "Just renting," he said. "It'll do. But be warned, it's messy."

They got the duffel out of the car, Bethany taking one end, Conner the other as he unlocked the front door.

"Wow. You weren't kidding," she said as they dropped the bag behind the sofa. "When was the last time you cleaned up around here?"

He shrugged as he shuffled past her—stepping around scattered piles of *Scientific American* and *National Geographic*, finance and tax trade journals, dusty furniture. He swooped up an empty beer glass from the coffee table on his way to the small square kitchen, averting his gaze from nearly a week's worth of dirty dishes piled in the sink. He reached into the fridge for a couple of diet sodas.

"I didn't know you'd be staying."

"Actually, it's totally fine," she said, appearing at the kitchen's entrance as he stood with the two soda cans. He held out one for her to take.

"Thanks." She popped the top and gulped. "Ryan," she sighed. "You wouldn't believe it. Turns out he's a mop and dust Nazi," she said, shaking her head. "At first, I was into it. Sorta, I guess. You know?" Her voice trailed upward in the way he heard so many young women speak these days. A language filled with question marks. "But I got sick of it and reverted to my slobbish ways. Which, of course, totally drove him nuts."

He sipped his soda. "So, just how serious is this rift? Have you decided to get a lawyer?"

She looked at him, drawing her mouth down and making her eyes big. It was a funny face of hers that always made him laugh before.

"Oh, Daddy..." She started taking dishes out of the sink, digging at smears of caked-on egg yolk with a thumbnail, putting them in the dishwasher sideways and backwards. Exactly opposite of how he did it. The sound of her voice, packed into those two words, was ragged and sad.

**

So, will you be my husband or my ex in the obit? Libby had teased him, her voice flat and dry. She had shaved her head and without her hair, her eyes had looked so much larger.

Even as Conner struggled to forgive her, he knew he wasn't the type to abandon a sick and dying wife. He teased her back, saying he'd crunched the numbers, that their assets were too entangled. He did not mention love or faithfulness, deciding instead to quietly put his old illusions to rest.

Who knew you could be so sentimental? she had said. He'd taken her hand in his, carefully, so as not to disturb the IV plunged into a vein trailing below her knuckles.

Oh, dammit, Conner. Why was I such an idiot?

He could be an idiot too, he assured her. But what was done was done. He had embraced the marital cliché of *in sickness and in health* as a newly-discovered truth. He had taken care of Libby with a measure of love that surprised him. During one especially difficult evening at the hospital in which she'd pleaded with him to stay the night, he gingerly angled himself into bed alongside her.

This is not a hospital bed. It's a meadow. Smell the air? Hear those birds? And I love you. she said.

He had felt himself melting at those words, then quickening. It had been so long since they'd shared a bed. Could love only be understood through the murky purgatory of failure?

Say it, she said.

This is not a hospital bed. It's a meadow. Smell the air? Hear those birds? he said.

And? she said. *And...?*

And...you love me.

✳✳

He stood waiting alongside a row of satin gowns—an avalanche of white. Bethany was trying on the shoes Trina had ordered for her. They were a pastel color. Lilac, she said. Trina's colors were lilac and celadon. Was he supposed to know what celadon is?

"It's that really pretty pale green shade, Dad, you know, like those Chinese vases they have in museums," she said as she studied the shoes in a mirror that held her reflection from the lower shins down. She returned them to the box, nodding to the clerk. As she rang them up, Bethany took out her wallet, thumbing through some bills.

"Geez, Dad, I'm nine dollars short and what?" She blinked at the register, then the clerk.

"Eighty-three cents," she said.

"Could you..."

Conner hesitated before reaching for his billfold. He pulled out a couple of fives and laid them on the counter.

She squeezed his hand. "Thanks. I'll pay you back. Promise."

He smiled. His daughter. She had her charms. They didn't always show. But she had them.

**

There was a second bedroom in the house, which Conner used as a home office. He furnished it with an old file cabinet and desk he found at a garage sale. Reams of copying paper were stacked alongside boxes of files. In a closet with a sliding door, he kept more files alongside computer cables, electric cords, some wire cutters, a couple of screwdrivers, and several boxes of checks which bore a ridiculously idyllic image—actually selected by Libby—of a duck pond with two ducks gliding serenely beneath his and Libby's names. The checks were useless now. He keeps meaning to shred them. Maybe one day, he'll get around to it.

"Who else has used the sofa bed?" Bethany said as she threw the shoe bag on top of her duffel before flopping onto the sofa's cushions.

"You'll be the first," he said. "It's new. Well, Salvation Army new."

Bethany folded her legs up against her, looking tired and restless as she glanced around the living room. She wrinkled her nose in disapproval. "You have no pictures hung. You need something. How long have you lived here?"

"A few months."

She held her hands out in front of her, inspecting her nails, shaking her head disagreeably before tucking them in her lap. "Gosh, Daddy, do you know, I figured out the length of my marriage in days? Still in the three figures," she said. "Nine hundred twenty."

He didn't know how to count days or years anymore. When someone said something had happened so many years ago, he often found himself unable to believe it. He no longer had any basic sense of time—how long an actual day was, or a week, or a month. Equally puzzling was how very long an actual hour could feel, or how quickly it could simply dissolve.

"Mom cursed my wedding," said Bethany.

Conner shook his head. "No, Beth. She didn't."

Libby had been older than Conner by five years. She told him when they got married that she was certain there'd be trouble and she'd likely be the one causing it. At the time, Conner laughed, telling her getting married always gives people a sinking feeling at first. He remembered his own surge of panic, standing with her before the justice of the peace. He too couldn't shake that small voice that kept telling him he'd lost his mind. Yet, like most people who were characteristically too cautious, Conner had thrown it all out the window when it came to Libby. He didn't care. Libby had taken staid, predictable Conner to the moon and back. She had made him feel like an exotic epiphyte instead of a well-rooted upright tree. It was the best ride he'd ever had, and that should have told him something. But, as always, such wisdom arrives too late, with its own lambent sting.

"Ryan thinks she was a sociopath," Bethany said.

"Oh, please..." Conner winced.

"I slapped him when he said that."

"Really?" said Conner.

"Really. I've never slapped anyone before. It surprised me," she said as she ran her fingers across her toes, like a pianist searching out a tune. "I guess that was the beginning of the end. Funny how these things happen."

**

Conner had met Libby at a friend's wedding. She was a distant cousin of his college buddy, Sam Mason, who was marrying Alice, a cousin of Conner's from his father's side of the family.

God, does that mean you're going to proposition me? He had laughed when she said this, which had made him realize he hadn't of late been laughing that much. But she had looked very serious when she said it. *It feels like some strange kind of cross-fertilization in the air, don't you think?* Then she smiled as she spooned caviar on her plate and fingered cubes of bright cheddar.

She was tall and slender, with striking gray eyes, dark hair that fell in spiraling tangles. *Maybe you should propose to me,* she had teased. And then she set her plate down, reached into her beaded handbag, took out a pen and a wrinkled gasoline receipt, quickly scribbled her phone number on it, and passed it to him.

Sshhh... she said, touching a finger to her lips.

To a man like Conner, clumsy when it came to women, cursed with thinking too much, Libby's boldness was disarming. With Libby, it had all been so easy. She had a beguiling, lazy charm that had less to do with beauty—though she was very pretty—than with a certain skillful frankness; ironic, playfully biting, and without the least bit of self-consciousness. He'd been insanely smitten. Desire pumped through his veins. Regrets be damned.

She was the daughter of a wealthy banker from Richmond, a fate that had shaped a rebellious spirit. Libby, Sam had warned him, was a girl willing to upend apple carts, a girl happy to stoke your illusions.

After passing him her phone number, he watched as she filled two champagne glasses and then, what couldn't have been more than a few seconds later, as a much older man dressed in summer seersucker and a bright pink shirt came and slid his arm around her waist. She passed him one of the champagne glasses as he kissed her on the skin below her ear before helping himself to a square of cheese from her plate.

Conner, meanwhile, had drifted furtively out of sight when the man appeared, but he still couldn't take his eyes off Libby as they wove their way around tables laden with tiers of carved, cubed, garnished, and decorated food. He had watched her tall body swaying as she led her shorter, lumbering companion by the hand, out beyond the food tent.

His heart was still beating wildly enough to drown out that

small voice of warning that this was trouble. That if someone like her wanted someone like him, something was wrong. But then again, maybe not. Coulomb's Law. It danced in his mind. Two interacting charges affected by a force that acts across the distance separating them.

Or, more succinctly, as Libby would call it—*good vibes.*

Besides, anyone's luck can change, he thought as he grabbed a plate and started happily filling it with food, suddenly ravenously hungry.

**

All day Saturday, Bethany cleaned. Cursing Ryan and cleaning the bathroom, cursing Ryan and vacuuming the floors, cursing while doing laundry—mostly hers. Conner watched, puzzled, insisting she needn't bother, but Bethany had brought with her a crazy energy of fickle unhappiness.

"Oh, gosh, I really don't mind, Daddy," she said, disturbingly cheerful. "At least this place could use a good cleaning."

But it made Conner nervous, watching her carom around the little house with dust cloths and brooms, a one-woman cleaning regiment. The smell of Pine-Sol was everywhere. It made him want to gag. When he tried gently to point out that this was an odd pattern for her, she just glared at him. Then, her phone would ring and she'd drop everything and plop on the floor and start talking about the seemingly endless details of Trina's wedding, how her own life was a slow-motion train wreck, how weird it was to be back home, and yes, she'd be here, staying with her dad for *a while.* She *had to help him out.*

He anxiously stroked his whiskers when he heard this.

On Sunday, late morning, Trina's wedding day, she stood at the kitchen sink, her hair wrapped in a towel, applying nail polish the color of Pepto-Bismol, one leg crooked, foot against thigh, wearing that same pair of denim shorts that showed her pale and freckled legs.

"You got a girlfriend, Dad?"

The question surprised him. "No," he answered, which was the truth. "I mean, well," he paused, "now and then I have the occasional date."

He'd dated since Libby's death. They were much like those before he met Libby, though he had discovered being a widower worked a little more in his favor. Yet, most of the women he knew were either in similarly confusing states of freedom or otherwise too occupied with busy careers to offer much beyond dinner or drinks, the heady promise of sex. There was Sheila, for instance, whom he'd met during his brief time in the apartment. But after a few dates, it began to take on the same pattern as others. Mild interest. Confounding lust. The lingering sense of disappointment.

"Why do you ask?"

Bethany kept brushing her nails as a smile slowly spread and she lifted her face, sliding her eyes to look at him.

"Oh, you know, just curious," she said, blowing on her fingers. "I came across a tube of lipstick in the bathroom." She shrugged. "Hope it's not a drag on your plans for me to be staying with you. You know."

"Ah." That lipstick. *Your mother's*, he wanted to say, but found he couldn't.

He raised a finger. "Um, Beth, honey." He paused. "Just how long are you planning, you know, to stay, anyway?"

She held her hands in front of her, fluttering her fingers, chewing the inside of her lip before looking up at him with that stung expression.

The doorbell rang. She jumped to get it, hurrying past him. She waved in two girls who were carrying bags and shoes and dresses sheathed in plastic. One, a redhead she introduced as Caitlin, the other, tawny and exotic, with dark upswept hair. Her name was Nema. They carried the heat of the summer morning with them. They've come to do Bethany's hair then it's off to the church. Bethany asked if they could use his bedroom so they could close the door. He heard their giggling, the fluid mingling of their voices, the occasional high-pitched note of what could either be enthusiasm or panic.

A half-hour later, they emerged. Bethany's hair braided, coiled and sleek, her face made up. She looked quite pretty, thought Conner, with a fatherly pang. The two young women wore long lilac-colored gowns, while Bethany's—as matron of honor, she had explained—was that celadon color. They stood at the doorway, a pastel trio, bustling and radiant. Bethany turned to him, waving before blowing him a kiss.

"I'll be in late," she said. "You know..."

"I know," he said, smiling.

It was two hours before the wedding. They had to swing by the florist to pick up their bouquets and get to the church so they could surround Trina (Caitlin referred to it as the pre-ceremonial triage) and, of course, Bethany had yet to see Trina's dress.

**

The evening was his. He was grateful to be alone. He could relax, kick back, watch some baseball.

He snacked in staggered intervals—chips and salsa, some leftover store-bought quiche, a few chocolate chip cookies. He downed three beers while absently watching the Nats lose to the Braves, then continued switching from an old movie channel to some dreadful British comedies then an entertainment news program where intrepid reporters stalked besotted celebrities like hunting dogs.

He finally nodded off, still sprawled on the sofa, naked feet on the coffee table. A few hours later, he awoke, stiff-necked, to the sound of gunfire, raising his head to see Gary Cooper, in grainy black and white, twirling a pistol. The house was dark except for the milky glare of the TV. He rubbed his eyes and the back of his neck, picked up the remote, and switched off the TV.

Bed, he thought. Ridiculous to have spent another evening falling asleep on the sofa, the TV blaring.

Bed. Where he hugged his pillow, aroused by feral longing. Occasionally, he awoke in the dark of night to what he thought were the sounds of someone walking in another room. But it was nothing more than cricket song, or the kind of creaks and taps and settling that a house makes.

When he slept on his side, the sound of his pulse filled his ears like the ticking of a clock. The bedroom felt larger, emptier, a rectangle floating away to nowhere. He exhaled Libby's name from the drifting landscapes of his dreams, scattering and vanishing, and he would awaken, feeling a weight like sandbags on his chest. The sound of his own quick breathing terrified him.

Now, as he leaned forward on the sofa, he felt a twinge in his back and groaned.

"Shit," he muttered as he rose to his feet. He stood in the warm darkness, his mouth dry and stale. On his way to the bathroom, he banged his big toe against Bethany's bag, cursing—a clumsy lapse suddenly reminding him that yes, his daughter was his houseguest, and, by the way, where in the hell was she? And why was she telling her friends *I'll be here for a while*, but not saying anything like that to him? No, regarding Conner, she ran around the house, hopeful with dust rags and disinfectant as weapons of endearment, clearly more interested in avoiding her problems with Ryan. And what better place to do that than here, with her father, a man living—no, drifting, really—from day to day, month to month?

He peed, ran a toothbrush around his mouth, all in darkness. He slipped out of his khakis and crawled into bed, surprised to see by the glow of his bedside alarm that it was after three in the morning.

**

He awoke to the raucous cries of a blue jay outside his window. And slants of sun on the carpet that signaled late morning. As he shuffled from bedroom to bathroom, he knew without having to check the living room that Bethany wasn't there. It must have turned into a long, celebratory night with old friends.

After showering, he looked at his face in the bathroom mirror. The whiskers were growing in pretty good now. Funny. He actually hadn't thought of having a beard. It happened as a result of his just not wanting to shave for a couple of days, and then he decided, why not?

He donned sweats and sneakers, put on coffee, and while the coffeemaker gurgled, he rearranged the dishes in the dishwasher. From time to time, he would lift the slat of one blind at the window over the kitchen sink and look outside to the driveway. Where was she? He felt a sudden awful shiver of fatherly dread as he took his phone in his palm and scrolled to her number, staring at it for a long moment.

She's fine, he thought. She's Bethany and she's fine. Sturdily, unhappily fine.

Should he let her stay? What would be the harm? The house was cleaner. That wasn't really so bad, was it? Didn't they, well...didn't they need one another? But it worried him. He didn't want to feel the tug of all that need again.

He busied himself, beginning with taking the paint scraper, which he used on the front door. Later, he'd go to the hardware store, pick out a new paint color. Maybe red? Libby would say go with red. Lipstick red.

His life now. Mostly celibate. Lust now expressed as a coat of red paint on a door.

A couple of hours later, while spreading mustard on a slice of bread and sniffing what was left of a package of deli turkey to make sure it hadn't turned, he heard the slamming of car doors, a squeal of girlish voices, farewell phrases dangling mid-air, and then the front door opening.

"Hey, Dad," she yelled. He felt a rush of relief.

She appeared in the kitchen, dressed in blue jeans and a T-shirt, looking considerably less glowing than yesterday. From her left hand, she dangled a large bouquet of wilting flowers trailing pink ribbons.

"Guess who caught the bouquet?" she said, raising it into the air, her mouth with that exaggerated pull downward.

He smiled. "How was it?"

She stood, turning the bouquet, examining it, fingering the ends of the ribbons wrapped around its stems.

"Oh, you know, it was..." She paused, then shrugged. "It was everything a wedding always is. You know. Sweet and fun. And sad."

She fussed with the flowers some more, cupping their heads to her nose, closing her eyes.

"Sad?"

She nodded. "Of course."

He thought of asking her where she had spent the night, but now didn't seem to be the right moment. Then she turned, walked out of the kitchen. He started after her, but stopped, craning his head around the kitchen's entry, watching her wander from room to room with the flowers. She finally settled on the couch, still holding the flowers close against her. She closed her eyes and lowered her head, the tip of her nose once again grazing over the petals, and then she started rocking back and forth.

He came and sat beside her. She shook her head, chuckling lightly.

"I cheated," she said. "I cheated on Ryan."

"Oh." He didn't know what to say.

She shrugged, looking at him. "I let a guy kiss me. Roger Kingston, from my senior year chemistry class. God, does he look better. We had some champagne, and some wedding cake, and we smooched. It was pretty silly, really. But I actually had a great time. I mean, I didn't exactly..."

He put a hand up. "No. Please. I don't want to know."

She frowned. "Oh, Daddy. I went home with Caitlin. Didn't you get my text?"

He shook his head. "Maybe somebody did. But it wasn't me."

"Ew." Her eyes got wide. "I did send you one," she said, blinking confusion before shrugging. "Anyway, I tried to get Trina to do a do-over on tossing the bouquet. She wouldn't. Thought it was bad luck. Then, Nema said she'd take it if I didn't want it, but then I decided I'd keep it after all. Crazy, isn't it?"

He nodded. "It's just a bouquet of flowers. A very over-priced one, I suspect."

She shook her head. "That is so not true, Daddy dear," she said. "Here, you take them." She thrust them at him, folding his hands around their stems. "Put them in a vase. Or not." She got up from the couch and trailed to the kitchen. He heard the refrigerator door open and close, the faucet running.

He looked at the flowers. He didn't want them. The house smelled bad enough as far as he was concerned. When she returned to the living room, he didn't hesitate. He tossed the flowers back at her. She let out a small yelp as she reached her hands out, seizing them mid-air.

She looked at him, surprised, a faint gleam of mischief in her eyes, a briefly-flickering holograph of Libby. She pitched the bouquet back to him. "I don't want it anymore," she said, laughing.

He leaped from the couch, grabbing the bouquet as it sailed at him upside-down, ribbons trailing, rose petals littering the carpet.

"I sure as hell don't want it," he said.

Bethany was laughing hard now, snorting and gurgling as she collapsed on the couch, burying her face in her hands. Conner sat back down alongside her, shaking his head, laughing too. She rubbed her face furiously with her palms, her cheeks flushed. She pounded her fists on her knees. He touched her hair. She rocked back and forth again, shaking her head.

"When, Daddy? When does it stop feeling so awful? So

different? It's like being on the dark side of the moon. I miss Mom. She ruined everything, but I just miss her. Like nothing can ever be the same. Ever."

⁎⁎

The dark side of the moon. Words like a knife in the heart. Libby in a dim hallway, its walls filled with paintings of tender landscapes in gilded frames, as she slips away from him again.

Wednesday morning and Conner stared at himself in the bathroom mirror, running a hand over the beard. It was thick, a moss-like scruff of gray and brown. He looked terrible. Really. Terrible. A backwoods madman with flabby muscles. He opened the medicine cabinet, reached for the shaving cream. Next to it was the small black tube of lipstick. The only thing of Libby's he had chosen to keep.

A reminder? A lesson?

Go back to your place, he had told Bethany. *I love you, but you need to go back. Don't run. Don't hide. Have it out with Ryan. Figure out what you want.* She had wept as he fixed her a sandwich. Tears, a little sustenance, and fifteen minutes later, she felt better. She rinsed her plate in the sink, and then she came up to him, gripping the sides of his face with her hands, squeezing his cheeks until his lips bunched up like a wadded tissue, imploring him to strike a deal. She'll go back if he'll lose the beard.

On Tuesday, a couple of hours after he dropped her off at the airport, he received a text from her: *Send me a selfie, post-shave! Xoxo.*

He filled his palm with a mound of white foam, spread it on his cheeks, his chin, his jawline.

You know what? Forget the lipstick. Libby had handed it back to him, along with the little round mirror she had asked him to bring her on one of her worst days.

Three hairs on the top of my head and a smile like a circus clown? No thanks.

He picked up his razor, placing it just below his left ear. He hesitated a second, or two, or three, before slowly gliding it until he glimpsed a smooth patch of skin, there, just below his ear.

Presence

I was in my kitchen pouring a glass of orange juice when I felt that peculiar light. Well, hardly anyone could have missed that aura—a shimmering pink-gold hologram. It took less than an hour after the green light on my 4×4" activation box began blinking, and there he was.

He was carrying the requisite paperwork: a copy of the procurement order from the county, with my signature; a copy of my doctor's assessment and consent. And a letter from Mr. Dexter Ramos, the Superintendent of Elderly Community Services, requesting from the manufacturer the particular *service emanation*, as they call them.

Everything looked to be in order.

"What should I call you?" I asked him.

He glowed with those nice gold and coral colors, making a dappled pattern on the floor. Was he trying to make a good impression?

"That is up to you, Mrs. Humphries. A number. Or a name. Whichever suits you."

I nodded. I liked the voice. It was quite close to what I wanted, though it did have just a trace of robotic inflection. Well, as Mr. Ramos explained, the voice thing is still a challenge.

I replied that I wasn't ready to decide about that just yet. I needed to spend some time with him. That seemed fine with him. He stood for another moment. Like a waterfall. Then, he excused himself and started wandering the rooms of my house, rustling the carpets, making his strange and shifting fields of colored light.

"Make yourself at home," I told him.

******

Here's the strange thing. He makes a sound like breathing. And he sighs. I like that. I've been alone for a while now. I'm eighty-five. Except for a few things, I manage okay for my age. I don't have children. Most of my closest friends are either dead or live far away. I live in one of the last small houses in my neighborhood. Cookie-cutter, they used to be called. It's the house where, in the early years of our marriage, my husband brought me home after two miscarriages; the house where we argued and mended one another; the house where he died. I can still feel the drift and eddying of our lives here in the floorboards I walk.

I missed Gerald. Especially those first years. But now I don't mind living alone. To tell you the truth, other people make me tired now. They try my patience. I guess I've become one of those "I love humanity but hate people" types.

I've grown weary of conversations where people don't listen, or don't really have anything to say, or it's clear they just like hearing themselves talk. And, well, I reluctantly admit I'm also a little deaf. So they shout at me. Like I'm a child that must be made to listen.

Hearing. Listening. They are not synonymous. You hear with your brain. You listen with your body.

But it pleases me that something like my programmed emanated assistant is in the next room.

He has an elusive yet solid presence. He quietly inhabits my house without the need for anxious conversation. He's just here. If I need him to do something, he comes and we get on with it. But otherwise, we don't say much to each other.

Haven't you ever passed a whole day with someone without speaking?

What is he? I haven't the faintest idea. Most of the time, he is an ever-changing color field. He makes footsteps I can hear. And when he gets near me, I can suddenly see the outline of a hand, a forearm, an upper arm, and the muscles of his shoulder. He actualizes a physical presence to help me out of my chair. Part of him becomes solidly physical and I can feel a hand beneath my forearm, guiding me, helping me stand and making sure I don't fall.

In the evenings, his colors change and he is like the blue dusk outside my living room window. Sometimes I've seen his chin, the outline of his head, his feet. I think he's playing with me when he does that (though Mr. Ramos says these service emanations aren't designed to manifest cheeky behavior like that. I wonder). Sometimes, he's a shadow, sometimes a mirror; he plays with my mind, as memories do. Ultimately, I suppose you could say he's nothing more than a collection of diaphanous pixels and that it's me, with my senses—my eyes and ears, my brain—that *assembles* him into what he is...at any given moment. But I'm not certain about that either.

Why do I say "he"?

Well, I did specifically request a male counterpart. Which means they gave my emanation a male voice and masculine demeanor.

I didn't want anyone I used to know or love. Not my husband, or either of my parents, or any long-gone aunts or uncles. Or my two younger brothers, whom I outlived. There's something about conjuring dead loved ones I couldn't bear. Not after having said goodbye. It invites too much in the way of judgment. And regret. I would feel all of the gaps and spaces in my life all over again.

I know. I know. That sounds like something else altogether, doesn't it? Something that's wrong. What would you call it?

A clinical term you would place the prefix *mal* in front of? I'm sure they have a name for it in some medical textbook.

They have a name for just about everything these days. But for me, that only deepens the mystery.

**

I mentioned how much I like his voice. It's because, despite my being nearly deaf, I can hear him.

His voice just finds my ear. I don't know what they did, how they tricked up the auditory resonance, but it works.

In the morning, he switches on lights to rouse me from bed. I call for him when I need help moving about, though I've told him I prefer to get around as much as I can on my own. After his first week, he took over my audio system, essentially downloading music from my CD collection so the music comes from him now. He just asks what I would like to listen to and there it is. And like his voice, I can hear the music. It's been a long time since I've been able to do that.

And yes, as I'm sure you're wondering by now, he does help me bathe and dress.

When I'm showering, he stands by, having discreetly blanched himself into a whitish glow waiting with a towel he holds like a butler balancing a silver tray on his fingertips.

That's a nice touch.

**

At night, I sometimes have pain in my calves or knees that keeps me awake. He'll come into my room and I can feel the aura of his hovering presence and he proposes a slideshow.

"Memory lane," he calls it.

"You're spouting clichés," I tell him. But that doesn't rattle him and the next thing I know I look up at the ceiling and there it is. A slideshow of memories.

He has shown me images of old photographs, and others, I don't know where they came from, of my wedding at the lighthouse in Maine (Gerald's idea; I wasn't as sure until it was all over), of my college graduation with me smiling stiffly (why? Nervous apprehension, most likely) and my parents smiling stiffly too, as if none of us could shake the feeling we didn't belong together; *Oh Mom, oh Daddy*, I moaned, seeing their faces like that again.

I asked how he did that and he explained it all comes from me. He merely had to *intuit* what to do. Which surprised me. I had no idea he was that fine-grained. I mean, intuition is a slippery thing, even for humans. He said he has access to a virtual warehouse of what he calls intuitive maps. He chooses them based on his interpretation of what my frame of mind is then *downloads* them as part of a pre-formulated internalization and transfer process he follows.

Not exactly mind reading, he explained.

******

One evening, I saw me, as a girl of five, dressed in white. A huge white bow pinned at an angle onto my dark, shoulder-length hair—my gosh, how young I was! I'm not smiling. My hands are folded in my lap. I was wearing those black patent-leather Mary Jane shoes, the white lace socks.

"Ridiculous bow," I said.

"Tell me more," he said softly, not ironically. "It is actually quite pretty."

I turned and looked at him—a cascade of floating, lavender light (he always chooses pastel shades for nighttime) out of which I could see the ghostly image of a pair of hands, folded much like mine were in the photograph.

"Pretty? You think it's pretty?"

The light shimmered and vibrated. "I do."

I threw my head back and laughed. He stayed quiet.

"My mother's idea. It was a big deal back then. I hated it. It took her a long time to get me dressed up like that. But she insisted. We were pretty good at wearing one another down. Of course, she always won. She had more practice than I did."

The feeling overcame me, remembering my mother and the ways in which she tried to *persuade* me about how to be. I felt tired thinking about it again.

"You are upset," he said, almost whispering. An effect that made the words sound louder.

"I'm tired," I said.

"You are also upset," he said.

"I think you got the wrong map," I said, in the same low-pitched voice he was using.

I looked at those hands and saw that he was tapping his left index finger over the top of his right hand. Was this a signal of ebbing patience?

Don't be silly, I thought. He sounds as patient as a nun. It's obviously me.

"Perhaps. It happens. Sometimes, our exactitude works against the situation," he said. "We will look at something else tomorrow."

I drifted off to sleep. The last thing I remember was how the room grew very dark and quiet and I knew, in a miasma of drifting weariness, that I was alone.

I didn't like the feeling at all. A few moments later, I felt him return. It's difficult to describe. The room was still dark, but it was filled with his presence. I could see only a faint, shadowy outline of him patiently sitting and waiting. Perhaps it was only my brainwaves or my longing for sleep, but I heard these words in my ear, clear and distinct: *I will stay with you until you are asleep.*

I became like a child again in sleep, my heartbeat like a pulsation inside a womb.

He's helped me get to sleep before. But never like this.

**

After a couple of weeks, we had gotten into a familiar groove with one another, though I still hadn't picked a name for him. One morning, he asked me about it. He said this in that nice way he always speaks to me. Not a trace of impatience.

Well, I had been thinking about it.

I had thought about Alan or William or James or Frank. Stephen, too. And, of course, Gerald. But it's tricky. I mean, I've known men with these names. My husband, as I mentioned. And my father. My brothers. A couple of friends from college days. To give him any one of those names is to see the person I used to know. I mean, for heaven's sake, I know there's more than one *Gerald* on this planet, but whenever I hear the name, whose face do you think I see?

I'm so foolish. I want to avoid what cannot be avoided.

"Just choose one," he said, glimmering near the stove, holding a frying pan mid-air. "You might remember but, after a while, you might forget too."

He set the pan down, turned the burner knob, and with a click, a blue flame appeared and I saw myself, eight years old, insisting that I wanted to strike the match and see it spark into a flame.

Paul? I thought. How about Paul?

My blue-eyed cousin Paul, three years older, and I was a little bit in love with him. We were in the old garden shed in my parents' backyard. It was a humid, boring Saturday afternoon. He'd come with some test tubes from a science kit, the matches, a handful of birthday candles, and a little bottle with some kind of liquid in it. We were mad scientists in our dingy lab, with a dirt floor, cobwebs, and a grimy window that hardly lct in the light.

He told me it would be better if he lit the match. But I stomped my feet and kept insisting. He relented and held out the candle as I dug a match from the box. After a couple of clumsy attempts, I finally got it and I remember feeling a rush of dangerous joy—like my thumb grazing a knife's edge—as I watched the flame bloom before I touched it to the wick; our breathing caused the match's flame to shudder, and we were giggling softly. When the wick took the flame, Paul sighed, his eyes wide. He nodded, whispering, "Good." He had tipped the candle sideways so I could light it, then as he tipped it again upright, I realized I'd put my other hand on his wrist. He didn't pull away; he just smiled at me and I remember smiling too, with what felt like my whole body, as I watched his face, lit by the flame, his eyes calm and beautiful. "Want to hold it?" he said. I nodded eagerly and our fingertips touched as he passed me the candle. He was about to open that little bottle of liquid when suddenly, the shed door creaked loudly and I gasped, startled. The candle slipped from my fingers as daylight flooded the dim space. My mother loomed, her nose wrinkling with disapproval. I turned to Paul and I think he saw the fear in my eyes; he quickly stomped out the candle and looked at my mother and said it was all his fault.

I stayed quiet.

I've never forgotten how he took the blame; my hand on his wrist, as if it knew it wanted to be there; our fingers touching. Six decades later, I stood at his deathbed, touching his hand again and remembering.

In the moment before that shed door opened violently, I had thought we were beautiful.

* *

"So," I told my emanation, "how about Paul?"

We were in the kitchen, where he was busy slicing an orange for my breakfast. When he heard the name Paul, he glowed and rippled. His aura seemed to expand, taking on all sorts of colors. I took that as a sign he liked the name.

Slices of orange floated to me on a plate. This was a small

ritual we'd begun recently and, I have to confess, I loved it.

"And shall I call you Chloe now?" he said. "Instead of Mrs. Humphries?"

It startled me to hear the sound of my first name. These days, almost everyone I know calls me Mrs. Humphries.

"Well," I said, "I suppose that's only fair. Isn't it?"

"You appear to be a little appre-hen-sive." His pronunciation of that word sounded a little clunky. I've discovered that occasionally he has trouble with words of more than three or four syllables. He puts the accent on the wrong syllable, or he'll pronounce a vowel that's normally silent.

"No need to worry about fairness," he went on, recovering his smoothness. "Are you sure it is okay?"

Did he really want to know? Or was he just activating one of his many algorithmic checklists?

"Well, Paul," I said, smiling because as I spoke the name, I saw my cousin and me again in that shed, playing with fire. "I think it's okay."

He glowed a bright orange, with glimmers of yellow and red, like a flame.

I lifted a wedge of orange to my lips. There he goes again, I thought as I sucked on the fruit. Playing with me.

**

So we became Paul and Chloe.

"Good morning, Chloe," he would say to me as he raised the shades in my bedroom.

"Good morning, Paul," I would answer.

At first, I liked it. And he was correct. After a few days of calling him Paul, I didn't immediately think of my cousin. The thought of him began to fade (though it never went away entirely). But something else crept in. From that realm of ephemeral light waves and algorithms *he* emerged. He was *Paul*. With a one-syllable, four-letter name, his presence grew in my mind, still an obliging and coolly polite colorscape, yet autonomous and possessed of something more than when he first arrived.

I also discovered I liked it when he spoke my name. He didn't botch the pronunciation. Hearing my name as I stirred from my bed in the morning made me feel as if I were present in a way I realized I hadn't felt in a long time.

I let him take over in the kitchen. Though I still liked doing a few things. Making my oatmeal in the morning, for instance. He seemed fine with that. He'd hover nearby, slicing fruit or spreading butter on bread as he glowed and rippled. I liked that. He would sit with me as I ate. I thought it was too bad he didn't eat food.

"It's so wonderful, just eating an orange," I told him one morning at breakfast.

He rippled, yellow and green and orange colors. "The texture of butter is interesting," he said.

I described things like apple pie, beef stroganoff, spaghetti, tuna fish salad.

Afterward, he would go around reciting the names of certain dishes and saying "yum" or "mmm...nice." It was amusing. Also unexpected.

One evening, I was watching a movie, an oldie from the black-and-white days of cinema. He was there, glowing in the way he would do when evening came. The movie was one of those maudlin Joan Crawford soap operas. She was one of the best when it came to making those crocodile tears. The scene came where she really had to turn on the waterworks and the next thing I knew, Paul was there, his aura pulsing quickly, attentively.

"She's crying?" he said. "But not really crying?"

"Oh, yes, she's good," I said.

He was quiet for a minute, then said, "Weeping? Another word for crying. Weeping is beautiful."

"Weeping?" I said. "Beautiful?"

"Don't you think?"

What was this? I thought, then shrugged it off. After all, in those old movies, they could make crying look like something beautiful. And Crawford had those big, dark eyes the cameras loved. Whenever she made tears, they glistened like diamonds.

I was about to ask him why he thought weeping was beautiful. I wanted to know his *thoughts*, as if he actually did have some. But then I looked at the center of that glowing, hovering aura that is him and saw the image of a TV set, a square, snowy screen that slowly coalesced into the faces of one beautiful actress after another, their eyes welling up and glistening. They were not clear images, but grainy, black and white.

"Pixilations of weeping," he said. "Nothing more than transmissions of light and shadow."

And with that, all those weeping faces dissolved into a shimmering gray field that briefly resembled a cloud before becoming *Paul* again.

For the first time, I reached out to touch him, but of course, my hand touched nothing. My knuckles glowed pink and orange and blue and he became silent, implacable as he softly breathed.

And I felt a rush of something...I don't know...something like...longing?

**

This void, this mere color field, began exhibiting odd little quirks. A weird curiosity and playfulness. He'd be stirring a pot of soup, for instance, and he'd bring the spoon to a mouth and slurp it a bit and then go "*mmmm...*"

Was he doing this to amuse me? Since that evening, watching that old movie, something had shifted. It was subtle, but he was different. Ripples of irregular function. Was it our being together, day in, day out?

One day, he announced he was going to make scrambled

eggs, but when he cracked the shell of an egg against the bowl, the egg landed on the floor instead. He kept doing this as I stood watching, speechless. There were half a dozen raw eggs on the kitchen floor and he just kept repeating "*scrambled eggs, scrambled eggs*," as his colors pulsated.

"Oh. A mess," he said.

Too much TV?

I thought of calling Mr. Ramos, but I hesitated, fearing they might recall him. He had a name now. He was Paul. He talked to me. I talked to him. I would fumble and waver and he'd help me. He would fumble and waver and I'd help him. Yes, I had begun to help him.

I had the sense he needed me. Mr. Ramos had told me the primary purpose of a service emanation was to be functional; useful as an auxiliary aid for my aging body and mind. And yes, to be able to simulate the provision of comfort, but comfort expressed in accordance with certain preset algorithms which had been determined based on a lengthy questionnaire I'd completed.

But this was different. My service emanation had flaws. He was becoming downright clumsy, dropping and spilling things.

One morning, he was slicing strawberries when the knife slipped and the strawberry went sideways before falling to the floor. I got up from the breakfast table to pick up the strawberry. As I tossed it in the sink, I saw two hands, fingers outstretched and tense. I started to fold a hand over his but it suddenly vanished, then I leaned into his aura and whispered into a cloud of shimmering colors that he needed to slow down, work more slowly. I felt everything grow still and quiet and dim. My skin dimpled with goosebumps. I felt my heart skip. But after a moment, he became a flickering prism, and my face was suddenly flooded with warmth.

"Oh," he said. "Of course."

**

After dinner one evening, I had dressed in my gown and robe and was washing my face. Outside, the wind started again. It had been doing that since late afternoon, but this time I could hear it, even with my half-deaf ears. As I was drying my face, I heard thunder.

"Paul?"

He didn't answer. I went from the bathroom through the bedroom and as I passed by my bedroom window I saw the tops of trees thrashing back and forth, leaves and branches blowing about.

"Yes, Chloe."

I breathed, relieved. He was in the hallway just outside my bedroom. Then another peal of thunder came, louder this time. The sky flashed too. I have always taken a strange delight in watching a storm.

"Come and see this," I said. "It's quite dramatic." I caught myself a second after I said this. He doesn't actually *see* anything.

Nonetheless, ever obliging, he came alongside me and as I turned to look at him, I was startled.

"Oh, my...gosh, Paul. Is something wrong?"

His color field had turned pale and grainier. He started to speak, but his voice carried like a faltering radio signal. Just as quickly, he "snowed"—white and dark grains coalescing into view. A whole body—arms, legs, feet, head; tall and slender and clad in black trousers and a white shirt, his mouth open, his eyes wide, his hands and fingers blinking to white-knuckled pain.

Another peal of thunder came, very deep and loud this time. I covered my ears with my hands. I spun around in time to see an illuminated vein of lightning pulsing into a long streak that spread above the treetops. It was beautiful.

I felt a flickering by my side, and the next thing I knew I

was standing in total darkness.

"Paul?"

Nothing.

The power had gone out, and Paul had disappeared with it.

The darkness was thick. Move, I thought. Just move.

Slowly, I started making my way to the kitchen, relying on that map in my brain that held the room-to-room pathways of my house. I knew trying to walk in darkness could create an unsteady confusion in someone my age. When I reached the hall outside my bedroom, I placed the palm of one hand on the wall to help me move from the hallway to the dining room and into the kitchen. Along the way, flashes of lightning offered brief, flickering glimpses of my progress.

What are you? I had once asked Paul in those first days after his arrival. He couldn't answer because of course he had no way of knowing himself. As himself. He said something about wavelengths of light and then gave me a lecture about light spectrums and something called *pattern interruptions* and I told him to stop because it was getting way too complicated for me.

Now he had left me, and yet seconds before he disappeared I had glimpsed him, a wholly intact corporeal (or was it?) presence wincing as if in pain.

I got to the kitchen and groped blindly in one of the kitchen drawers for a flashlight and a candle, then fumbled near the stovetop for the box of matches before remembering I had the flashlight. I laughed. Heavy rain pelted the roof.

"Paul," I whispered in the dark.

Already, I missed him.

I sat at the table, remembering that morning he sent slices of orange floating to me on a plate as I waited.

I struck a match and lit the candle, one that was larger than the birthday candle my cousin and I used that day in the shed. I tilted it toward a little saucer, letting some wax drip and collect into a blob I could set the candle in and as I did, I was a girl again, living in a long-ago world where toy animals were carved of wood, not pixels; a tactile place of touch and smell and ticking clock faces; of powdery nubs of chalk pecking formulas on a blackboard. A world of minerals and earth and the smell of animals. I remembered what Gerald once told me about silica and how the world really is in a grain of sand. But I never imagined it could breathe and glow.

From across the dark kitchen, lit only by that candle, I saw the green light from the activation box suddenly blink awake. I heard the rain falling steadily and rhythmically. I held my arm to the candlelight and ran my finger along a path of blue veins that I could see and feel through my thin, creped skin. They branched like the shape of lightning.

Something faintly shimmered near the box, like little halos coalescing.

"Paul?" I whispered. "Paul? Is that you?"

Acknowledgments

I am grateful to the editors of the journals and anthologies in which the following stories included here, with minor modifications, first appeared: *Geographies* first published in *Avatar Review* (June 2008) and subsequently selected to be included in the anthology *Best of the Web 2009* (Print), published by Dzanc Books; *The White Cliffs Hotel* first appeared in the journal *Wanderlust* (Winter 2010); *A Bowl Full of Oranges* first appeared in *Lindenwood Review* (Spring 2015, Print); *High Grass* appeared in *Barrelhouse* (October 2015, Online); *Needles* first appeared in *Noctua Review* (April 2018, Print and Online); *Without A Map* first appeared in the annual anthology *Grace and Darkness* published by Gargoyle Press (May 2018, Print); and *The List* first appeared in *Rathalla Review* (November 2021, Online and also selected to be included in their annual print edition published in the Spring, 2022).

The lines by Louise Glück are taken from her poem *From the Japanese* and those of Carl Sandburg's are from his poem *Love is a Deep and a Dark and a Lonely*.

My heartfelt thanks to my wonderful group of fellow writers who, over the course of many years, read these stories and offered their invaluable guidance and insightful comments, always with honesty and generosity, humor and wisdom: Catherine Bell, Jim Beane, Dana Cann, Christina Kovac, James Mathews, Madelyn Rosenberg and Kathleen Wheaton. These stories would never have seen the light of day without them.

Special thanks to the DC Women Writers group and the Writer's Center in Bethesda, Maryland for providing refuge, friendship and connection, and to Trudy Hale who offered a room with a view and splendid peace at her retreat The Porches, in Norwood, Virginia.

Thanks also to my team at Atmosphere Press for smoothly guiding me through the process of publication from raw manuscript to finished product: my Developmental Editor, Tina Cane, who offered helpful guidance in the shaping of this collection; my Art Director, Ronaldo Alves, and his graphic design team for helping me make a beautiful cover; and my Managing Editor, Alex Kale – patient, kind and super efficient.

I wish to acknowledge, with deep sadness, the passing this year of my eldest brother, Woodrow who possessed such a remarkable creative spirit. So many years ago – before I even knew who I was – he lit a spark in me simply by showing what he could do with a graphite pencil and that the power of mere possibility and determination can be magical.

Finally, I want to thank my husband, Daniel, who read many of these stories and offered valuable suggestions and comments as well as many technical and grammatical corrections and whose unfailing love, encouragement and support over the course of so many years has helped me keep my dream alive.

About Atmosphere Press

Founded in 2015, Atmosphere Press was built on the principles of Honesty, Transparency, Professionalism, Kindness, and Making Your Book Awesome. As an ethical and author-friendly hybrid press, we stay true to that founding mission today.

If you're a reader, enter our giveaway for a free book here:

SCAN TO ENTER
BOOK GIVEAWAY

If you're a writer, submit your manuscript for consideration here:

SCAN TO SUBMIT
MANUSCRIPT

And always feel free to visit Atmosphere Press and our authors online at atmospherepress.com. See you there soon!

About the Author

CARMELINDA BLAGG was born in Oklahoma and grew up in Texas and, after earning her B.A. in English from the University of Texas at Dallas, she traveled throughout Europe, living for an extended time in Italy and France. After returning home, she resettled in the Washington, D.C., area where she worked for the World Bank for fifteen years. While working, she earned her M.A. in Writing from Johns Hopkins University and, after retiring, she began pursuing her longtime dream of writing. She has published her short fiction in many journals and anthologies, both online and in print, and in 2010, she was awarded an Individual Artist Award from the Maryland State Arts Council. She presently resides in Washington, D.C. This is her first collection of stories.